Bob Moats

Dark
Carnival
Murders

By Bob Moats

1

Dark Carnival Murders

This is a work of pure fiction. Names, characters, places, and incidents either are the product of the author's imagination or are used fictitiously, and any resemblance to actual persons, living or dead, business establishments, events, or locales is entirely coincidental.

ISBN – 978-0-9903138-5-4

For information and address:
Magic 1 Productions
P.O. Box 524, Fraser MI 48026-0524
Website: http://murdernovels.com
Cover by Bob Moats

Bob Moats

Jim Richards series books by Bob Moats

(In Series Order)
Classmate Murders
Vegas Showgirl Murders
Dominatrix Murders
Mistress Murders
Bridezilla Murders
Magic Murders
Strip Club Murders
Made-for-TV Murders
Mystery Cruise Murders
Talk Show Murders
Sin City Murders
Black Widow Murders
Vegas Vigilante Murders
Area 51 Murders
Mortuary Murders
Hypnotic Murders
Sunshine State Murders
Blue Suede Murders
Honky Tonk Murders
Dark Carnival Murders
Lipstick Murders
Pasta Murders
Talent Show Murders
Shyster Murders
Campground Murders
Network Murders
Reunion Murders
Big Apple Murders
Kennel Murders
Trick or Treat Murders
Santa Murders
Wiseguy Murders

For a preview or to purchase a book, go to
http://murdernovels.com

What a few people are saying about Murder Novels by Bob Moats

Mr. Moats, I just got your novel "Classmate Murders" and have to let you know, I read it in one evening. That is the first book I have ever done that with. That was the most enjoyable book I have ever read. I just started reading e-books, and reading again, after getting my wife a Kindle. This book was my 12th, and the best. I just got Las Vegas Showgirls to (read) tomorrow evening. I look forward to reading many of your books in this series. I have been searching for an author and books that were fun, entertaining reads. Your books are just the ticket.

Regards, A new fan, Bill from South Carolina

****

Another very nice comment submitted through my website from Micki P.:

"I recently was given a kindle for my 60th birthday. The first book I downloaded was the Classmate Murders and have now read every one of the them. Today I started on the Fatal Rejection series. Thank you for the wonderful ride with Jim and Penny and all the rest of the troop. I have laughed and giggled thru the stories, my poor family gave me the strangest looks! Now I really want a little Yorkie!! Fatal Rejection so far is another great read! I will be looking out for more of Jim Richards and since you are my #1 Author, anything of yours I can find."

Extra special thanks to:

Special thanks to Val Brooks who edited this book and for her great suggestions.

Thank you to all the people who purchased this book. I hope you enjoy it as much as I enjoyed writing it for my faithful readers.

The Jim Richards Family of Readers is listed in the back of the book.

Dark Carnival Murders
By Bob Moats

Chapter 1

They slowly moved in under cover of the pale moon. Enough light to see what they needed to do; but not enough to attract much attention. The convoy of trucks pulled into the center of the expansive twenty acres of still untouched desert land. In one corner of the property sat construction equipment and supplies to soon build the most expensive and most glamorous towers of condos in Las Vegas, but the work had been delayed while the investors battled over profit division.

The trucks came to a stop in formation for the building of another type of attraction; the men flowed out of the cabs and started to pull out equipment and parts to build the rides on which people would find thrills and chills.

A huge tent went up at the perimeter where the rides were being set up and a gaily colored banner was strung across the front of the tent where it could be seen easily from the road. It read "Jacob S. Dark's Traveling Carnival and Wonder Shows."

Three hours later, the tent was equipped with all that was needed to amaze and amuse the crowds with the greatest sideshow of geeks and freaks found on earth.

From the edge of the lot, two young boys were watching the activities. They had told their parents that they were camping in the backyard in the pup tent they had set up. But the flyer they had found blowing in the street summoned them to the lot where a bigger tent and rides were growing before them. So when it was finally dark, they'd snuck out of the yard and walked the mile from their home to the place where they knew magic would happen. They quietly moved up to the back of the tent and listened carefully at the canvas.

Suddenly a flap in the tent opened and there stood a tall, dark man, in a black suit, the type a funeral director from the western movies would wear. Tall stovepipe hat, a pencil thin mustache and he had what the hip folks on the strip would call a soul patch beard.

The boys froze, one felt a trickle of wetness running down his leg, the other just made a small yelp. The man smiled and said loud and boisterously, "Welcome boys, don't be frightened, this is my carnival and you can come in to help set up the side shows and the games of chance. I pay well, and you get to go on the rides for free. Just step on in and I'll take care of you."

The older boy looked to the other and nodded, then they happily ran into the tent. The tall, dark man grinned, looked out to the vast area to see if anyone was watching, and then slowly closed the flap.

~~*~~

It was Saturday morning and I wanted to sleep in, so I had already warned my beautiful wife Penny not to disturb me under penalty of death. I, of course, couldn't sleep so I just stared at the ceiling as Willy, our tiny toy Yorkie licked my foot hanging over the edge of the bed. I usually slept in strange positions but my leg over the side of the bed was not one of them. Moreover, Willy's tongue tickling my foot wasn't on my list of favorite things.

I gave up and swung my other leg over the bed causing Willy to rush out of the room before I could trample him. I stood and stretched, went to my bathroom and started my day.

A half-hour later I came out to the kitchen, but it was empty. No Angelo, no Penny. Odd, I thought and saw the patio door was open. I went out and stopped by the ugly Greek God statue that still occupied the patio, reached down into the can at the foot of the statue and pulled a handful of feed, throwing it into the Koi pond in front of the statue. The huge goldfish devoured the pellets and I ventured on past them. I could smell food cooking and went to the backyard and found Angelo and Penny at the incinerator, which is what we called our BBQ.

"Smells great, what's cooking?" I asked.

"What are you doing up? I thought you wanted to get some sleep?" Penny asked.

"Willy kept waking me," I said with a grin.

She walked over and gave me a kiss, then said, "Sure, blame the pup. You just couldn't sleep in on such a beautiful day. Angelo decided to make breakfast burritos and he asked if he could cook on the grill for the meat, onions and peppers."

"Good morning Mr. R. I'll have these ready shortly," Angelo said as he was flipping the foods on the skillet.

"Thank you Angelo, it smells great." I turned my attention to Penny and continued, "I hope Lynn and Deacon are enjoying their honeymoon," I said, talking about our friends finally getting married a week ago, it was a good ceremony, then Penny and I sent them to Hawaii for their honeymoon. "I checked the online weather in Hawaii and they have no monsoons or volcanic activities."

"And as long as there are no murders, they should be happy," Penny offered as we sat on the picnic table watching Angelo do his magic with food.

"What are we planning on doing today?" I asked.

"I was reading in the Review-Journal that there was a carnival in town, I haven't been to one in years, shall we go there?" Penny said with a hopeful look.

I thought back to my hometown in Michigan and the carnival that would set up every year behind my parent's home. "I used to go help get the side show games set up when the carnival came to my town years ago. It was fun to be around and they would give me tickets to go on the rides free. I think it's a good idea."

"Good, because I already invited Angelo to go with us."

"Sure of yourself, eh? What if I said no?"

"I would have taken Angelo and went anyway." She stuck her tongue out and stood as Angelo said the food was ready.

We gathered our soft shells and spooned on the ingredients, rolling them to eat. "Angelo, you're Italian, where did you learn to make Mexican food?" I asked.

"When I was young, mom had a cook on the estate that was Mexican and she taught me," he said with a laugh.

"Your grandmother had a restaurant and taught you to cook, now you tell me you learned to make Mexican treats. You should open a restaurant and call it ItaliMex. It would be something different," I said.

"Angelo, how is Francis doing?" Penny asked.

"Mom still calls me every couple days. I miss her but I had to get away from the family life. Being a enforcer for the mob was not something I wanted to do all my life. I like it here and as we talked about, I may still open a restaurant."

"What about the bodyguard work you're doing for Buck?" I asked.

"I like that but I need something more creative, food has always been a passion of mine," he replied.

"Thankfully for us," Penny whispered to me.

"Yes dear, I'm very thankful you don't have to cook." She whacked my arm, I was getting used to it by now.

We finished our breakfast and went in to finish getting ready for the day. My cell phone buzzed and Penny gave me an evil eye.

"If that's a murder case, forget it," she said.

"The caller ID says it's Earl," I told Penny and answered it.

"What's up chief?" I said and put it on speakerphone.

"Just wanted to see what you guys are up to, we haven't gotten together very much since Paula and I have been out here," he said.

I looked to Penny and she said to me, "Ask them if they want to go to the carnival?"

Earl heard her and said, "Carnival? I love carnivals. Where is it?"

"Out south of the strip in the area where they are doing all the new construction. The property is still open desert land and the thing is being sponsored by some community group to give a good family spin on Vegas. Interested?" Penny said.

"Sure, shall we come meet you at your place?

I spoke, "No, go to the office, it's just up the road from where they are set up, we can meet there."

"Sounds good, how soon?"

"We're getting ready to go now, see you shortly," I said and hung up.

We gathered everything we would need to start our journey; Angelo met us in front by the van.

"Gee, Mrs. R. I haven't been to a carnival in years. Last time, we had to run out because the Feds were after my late father."

Dark Carnival Murders

Penny was trying not to laugh, and got in the van and buckled up. We were all seated and I drove to the office on Industrial Road. It was about three miles from the desert area that would soon be a luxury complex of condos for the rich, now inhabited by the carnival.

I pulled into the parking lot of the office and saw Earl talking to a man and woman. I pulled in and parked. Earl waited until Penny, Angelo and I got up close, and then introduced the people.

"Jim, this is Mr. and Mrs. Walker, they just pulled in before you and they told me they have a problem."

The man came forward and held out his hand to shake, I took it. "Mr. Richards, we need your help. The police can't help us right now. Our boys are missing, they were supposed to be camping in our backyard, but early this morning we found they were gone. We don't know where they could have went to, but we found this in the tent." He handed me a folded yellow sheet of paper.

I opened the folded sheet and read the announcement about the carnival coming to town. I had a feeling this was going to be interesting.

*

Chapter 2

I hadn't planned on opening the office, but invited everyone in. I had them all sit in the waiting area, mainly because the couches were more comfortable than the chairs in my office and because there were too many people.

I said hi to Paula, I hadn't seen her in since Lynn and Deacon's wedding and then asked everyone to sit.

"Mr. Walker, you said the police can't help?" I asked.

"They told us it was too early to have them classified as missing; they could have just wandered off. But our sons would never just wander off. We are concerned, this is not something they would do."

I thought back to all the crazy things I did without telling my parents. "I can understand your concern, do you think they might have gone off to this carnival?"

"We were hoping it was just that, but we

went by the carnival and didn't see them anywhere. We showed pictures of our sons to a couple of the carnival people, but they said they hadn't seen them. We went to the police then, but where told to wait till later to see if they return."

"Maybe they will, but tell you what, we were planning on going to that carnival today, so maybe my associate and I could do some snooping and see what we can find, how's that for now?"

"We'd appreciate that, Mr. Richards, I don't have a lot of money but we could pay you for your efforts."

"No you won't, we're just happy to help. We'll go take a look and let you know what we find. If we could borrow the pictures of your sons, that may help also." He pulled out a picture of the two boys together and handed it to me. I studied the faces of the two boys, they looked halfway intelligent. "What are their names?"

"The older one is Keiran and the younger is Douglas," the mother said.

"Good this picture will help. Now I think you should go back home in case they come back and find that you aren't there."

The father looked shocked at the thought
16

there was no one at their house. "Oh God, I didn't think of that. Thank you." He stood and took out a business card and handed it to me. "We'll wait to hear from you." They left as I looked at the card.

"He's a furniture salesman. Maybe we can get a discount on some new office furniture," I said with a laugh.

Penny came over to me and said, "I hope you can find the boys; that's so sad when children disappear."

Earl came up and said, "They're probably just exploring the carnival, then they went home and found that their parents had ran off on them."

"Either way, we need to be on alert," I said as I made copies of the picture on the office copier and gave one to Earl and Paula, then one to Angelo. "Keep your eyes open."

We all went back out to our vehicles and I led them out on Industrial Road, and then snaked the way down to Tropicana, cutting over the freeway to Las Vegas Boulevard. I turned south and drove past McCarran International Airport. I had always loved watching the huge passenger planes coming in low across the highways landing from destinations unknown. I drove down the two-way divided highway past the famous "Welcome to Las

Vegas" sign across from the airport; which was technically the end of the Vegas "Strip" of casinos and hotels, just south of the Mandalay Bay Hotel.

I continued down South Las Vegas Boulevard passing small malls and restaurants, then past the mammoth Las Vegas Premium Outlet Center where Penny dragged me to a couple times a month. Although I did enjoy visiting this huge mall, there were plenty of adult toy stores for me to explore.

I drove on, Earl was keeping up with my van and then about four miles from the end of the strip we came up on East Silverado Ranch Boulevard and the Cinemark Century 16 movie theatre, so I knew we were close.

I drove a little further south to where the land was getting more open and less populated by businesses. I could see ahead just past W. Frias Road, where the cars were turning on to the desert land and up to the carnival. It was a bit crazy for parking; they had no system for lining up the cars, so people just parked where they could. Earl and Paula pulled up next to me and they got out. Penny, Angelo and I got out and went to our friends.

It was hot on the dry, dusty desert land, there was no breeze, just dry heat. Penny had a two of those little handheld battery operated fans and gave one to Paula.

"None for me?" I asked.

"You can stay hot, I may need it for later," she said with an evil smile.

"Sure, that's all I'm good for, keeping you warm," I said as we headed for the midway.

We entered the edge of the layout of rides and walked down one row watching all the people, mostly kids, screaming as they were flying or hurtling through space on an assortment of high-powered amusements. When I was a kid I always enjoyed the Tilt-a-whirl, but as I got older I discovered I would suffer from extreme motion sickness. So spinning rides were out for me.

We arrived at the end of the row of rides and I said, "Angelo, would you escort the ladies around the grounds while the super-spy and I go see if we can find the missing boys."

"It'd be my pleasure, Mr. R.," he said with a grin.

Penny gave me a kiss and said, "Don't go getting yourselves kidnapped."

"I won't, that's your job." Earl and I left our

group and went in the direction of the sideshow tent. We stopped outside the main entrance as I said, "When you were a kid and went to the circus, how did you get in to see the show?"

Earl laughed and said, "I snuck in under the tent in the back."

"Good to see your childhood wasn't wasted," I said and he followed me off to the side to see what we could find around the back.

It was deserted and dusty behind the tent looking out to the vast flat property only to see the freeway in the distance with cars whizzing by.

"The boys had to cross over the freeway to get here from the subdivision on the other side. Let's see if we can find any footprints in the sand." We walked away from the tent and did a sweep but there were a number of prints in the sand, probably from the carnies working. I did see a couple smaller prints that came in from the freeway and headed straight for the tent, I pointed them out to Earl and we followed them back.

We were just up to the back of the tent when we heard a voice, "I hope you two aren't thinking of sneaking in?"

We looked over to see a fairly tall man in a

black topcoat, wearing a tall top hat. He reminded me of pictures of Mephistopheles, one of the chief demons of European literary. He was holding a flap to an opening in the tent, where the footprints led to. "May I help you gentlemen?" he inquired smoothly.

He took both of us by surprise; he made no sound to warn us of his presence. I reached back and pulled my P.I. ID wallet with the auxiliary LVMPD police badge that Lynn gave me back when Weber had her deputize me during the search for a dirty bomb last year, they never asked for it back.

I held it out briefly so he got a glimpse of it, not saying that I was police, and then said, "We're investigating the disappearance of two young boys." I took the photo out of my pocket and went to him, holding the picture up where he could see.

"Sorry, I see hundreds of boys, after a while their faces all blend together. But I'll remember these faces and if I see them, I'll call the police."

He stepped back in, pulled the flap closed and was gone. "That was strange," Earl said. "He looks like a character from a Marvel comic, you know the evil type."

"Yeah, someone from a kid's nightmare." I

went to the flap but it was somehow secured from inside. "I'd like to see in this tent. Think they'd get upset if we broke in?"

"Well, you started it and he never said we couldn't come in," Earl laughed.

I was able to reach in the flap and found a strap holding it closed. I managed to release it and pull the flap back. "Okay, now we break and enter."

It was dark but there was a little light from above, there was a narrow walkway with wall of canvas all along the back of the tent with boxes and crates piled along the row. There were narrow openings between what I presumed were stages built off the ground. We went to one opening and found ourselves staring at faces staring back at us. It was the sideshow and we were between the bearded lady and a rubber man. I looked to Earl and laughed, then we went through the opening to where the audience was standing. All along the back of the tent were small platforms where geeks and freaks performed for the delight of the patrons.

Earl and I were standing watching some geek stick sharp rods through the skin of his chest, I was cringing when I felt someone standing too close behind us. Earl and I both looked back into the chest of a very tall and well-built man, he stood about two heads taller than us.

The giant looked down to us and growled, "You two need to leave. Now!"

     *

Chapter 3

The huge man grabbed both of us by the necks, his giant fists clamping almost all the way around them. Earl went into his black ops mode, grabbed the thumb of the man and tried to bend it back. The man was strong but Earl used leverage and managed to force the giant to release him and twisted his arm back enough to cause the giant to fall back to the ground. He had released me and I pulled my Glock out and stuck it in his face.

"Physical assault, not a nice thing," I said to him. He just laid there not moving as Earl released his thumb lock. People around us weren't sure if this was part of the show but started to applaud. Earl and I took our bows and went out the exit of the tent. As we went out, the man in the hat stood before us.

Dark Carnival Murders

"Gentlemen, while I have every respect for law enforcement, you must not break laws either. You have to pay to gain entrance like everyone else."

I pulled a five from my pocket and stuck it in the top pocket of his coat. "Here, keep the change. We're looking for two missing boys, and we will do what it takes to find them. So don't get in our way Mr. what-ever-your-name is."

He tipped his hat and said, "It's Dark, Jacob S. Dark. I own this show, and I'll cooperate with you in finding the boys, just consult with me first." He replaced his hat, scowled at us and sped off.

"As Alice said, 'curiouser and curiouser'." Earl said to me.

"I didn't know you knew the classics?"

"I'm a reader, everything but your books. They bore me to death," he said with a grin and walked away.

I yelled, "What?" then I followed.

We walked around the midway watching for the boys and showing the picture to people we passed. We hit every ride and showed the photos to the carnies who operated the rides, we got nada.

"Okay this is turning out to be a bust," I said and pulled my cell phone and the card that Walker gave me. I dialed his home number and he came on after the first ring. I could tell he was on edge.

"Mr. Walker, it's Jim Richards, I don't suppose the boys came home?"

"No, have you found out anything?"

"We're still at the carnival and haven't found anyone who recognized them. Could they have gone somewhere else besides the carnival?"

"I really don't know, they have never gone off on their own before. It's not something they would do. Oh God, I hope they weren't kidnapped from their tent," he said with a shaky voice.

"I would think by now that kidnappers would have called you, so let's rule that out for now. All we have is that they wandered off from their tent and could have come here. We aren't finished searching so sit tight and I'll get back to you." He thanked me and I hung up.

"I really hate not knowing where someone or something is. Like trying to find your keys, you thought they were on the table but now they aren't," Earl said as I put my cell phone away. "Well, where to now?"

"I don't know, maybe we could look around all the trucks that brought the carnival here," I said.

"Works for me, I'd like to meet that giant again without the public around."

"You're so macho aren't you?"

"Hey, it's been way too long since I killed a man with my bare hands."

"Or overthrew a government, yeah, yeah," I laughed.

We went to the area were all the big rigs were parked and wandered around listening for any sounds that might be boys locked in a truck. We heard no banging or Morse code to give away their location and stopped at the end of the row.

"Short of breaking in a few of the enclosed trucks, we got nothing. I don't want to incur the wrath of LVMPD by breaking and entering locked vehicles, if we got caught. So now what?" Earl asked.

"Maybe we should talk to Lynn and see what LVMPD can do for us," I said.

I pulled my cell phone and called Penny, "Where are you?" I asked after she answered.

"We're in the beer tent having a few cold ones," she replied.

"Save one for me, we're on the way." I hung up and we went back to the midway and over to the beer tent. I saw Angelo first; he was easy to spot in a crowd because most people just moved away from him. He just screamed Mafia from his looks, kind of like the Sopranos on TV. Earl and I got a couple beers at the counter and went to the picnic table where they were seated.

"No luck?" Penny asked.

"We got to meet the owner of the place and a very huge giant that we wrestled to the ground," I said.

Earl spoke up, "I wrestled him to the ground, you just stood peeing your pants after he grabbed your neck."

"I did no such thing. I had my gun on him while you were rolling around holding hands with him, did he give you his phone number?."

Penny and Paula both were laughing and then

27

Penny said, "Great, so you didn't find the boys?"

"No, I think we may have to call Lynn in on this, it may be too soon for missing persons, but they are seriously gone and may need police intervention to get into the inner sanctum of this place. I still believe they came here," I said.

"Mr. Dark seemed too cool about the picture you showed him, he's hiding something," Earl said and took a big swig of his beer.

"Yes he did, no concern or sympathy from a man who entertains children of all ages," I said.

"And he's spooky," Earl added.

"Problem is, Lynn would need some facts before she can get a warrant in to investigate. I think I may have an idea," I said and took a swig of my beer; it was chilled and tasted good in the hot tent.

"Okay, what is your idea?" Penny asked after I said no more.

I smiled and said, "I'll tell everyone after I talk to Buck."

We enjoyed the festivities and then stopped for the day. It was getting too hot to be out of reach of an air conditioner.

We all left the carnival, I watched it in my rearview mirror, it started to look evil. I drove back to the agency, Earl and Paula went to the lobby couches to watch TV followed by Angelo, as I went to my office to call Buck, explaining to Penny that there was little time to waste to find the boys, she agreed.

Buck answered after a couple rings and I told him who I was.

"Jimmy, how's your day going?" he asked.

"Well, it could be better; I need your help if you aren't doing anything?"

"Maria is sleeping, she has to work tonight and I'm just sitting here watching monster trucks on TV. Whatcha got going?"

"Can you come into the office and I'll explain. Also if you could see if Mac is free, I'll need both of you."

"I'll be in shortly after I call Mac," he said and hung up. I sat back in my office chair and smiled to Penny.

"How are you going to use Buck and Mac?" Penny asked.

"Tell me what you thought of Buck, since the first time you met him during the classmate murders?"

"I thought he was a big biker and tough, he was scary at first but I grew to know how much of a teddy bear he is."

"Yes, but that teddy bear can become a grizzly if poked. That's what I need right now."

"You're going to send him into the carnival, him and Mac as undercover, am I right."

"You are one smart babe," I said with a smile.

We went out to where everyone else was relaxing in the cool air of the office. Penny went to sit next to Paula as they were watching Saturday cartoons on the wide screen television. Educational TV, I guess.

About thirty minutes later Buck came in followed by Mac, Lacey and their adopted teenage daughter Jessie. I cringed that Lacey came in, it meant having to explain to her that I needed her husband for a couple days. I invited Earl, Buck,

Mac and Lacey to my office, asking Jessie to sit with Penny and Paula to watch cartoons, she liked that.

They were sitting around my desk while I was still standing. I put the photo of the missing boys on the desk in front of Buck and Mac.

"These boys went missing early this morning, we think they went to the big carnival south on Las Vegas Boulevard by Silverado Ranch Boulevard. Earl and I explored the carnival and didn't find them, but we suspect there is more than what the people who work there are telling. We met the owner, a real evil kind of guy and he wasn't very helpful. We couldn't do much in the way of searching the place without breaking the law. I had an idea that may help, but it involves going undercover." I paused for it to take effect.

Buck was mulling it over and said, "So you want Mac and me to join the circus?"

"Carnival, but same difference, yes. I need someone inside to see what evil is in the place," I said. "Just to be on the safe side I want to send both of you in, they may take one or both of you."

It was quiet for a moment, then Lacey asked, "Do they get overtime?"

Chapter 4

I smiled at Lacey and said, "I glad that you're worried about your husband's safety over money."

"Crap on that, we need finances to take care of bills," she replied.

I thought about it and said, "Do you need a raise, Lacey?"

"It would help us, Jessie is almost a teenager now and she needs things, women things."

"Okay, we can discuss this Monday. I'm open for a raise," I said knowing that we had the money to give her more of it. I wasn't greedy, ask my wife.

"Now can we get back to the case at hand? I need you two to go in and get a job with these people and let us know if there is any criminal activities going on and see if you can find the boys."

"I like it," Buck said and looked to Mac, "How about you?"

"I'm game, when do we start?"

"We need to get you two out there as soon as possible. The longer we wait, these boys may be in more serious danger. Earl and I both think there is more going on and we can't drag Lynn in without some proof. You'll have to dig something up. Now we have to build a back story for you to tell them."

Buck spoke, "I worked one summer at the old Bob-Lo amusement park south of Detroit. So I got some experience."

"I remember Bob-Lo, the island between Detroit and Canada. I went there one time years ago on the boat. That's good, Mac you have anything?"

"I did three weeks at a State Fair in Kansas City working all the rides. I can pass any test they throw at me," Mac said.

"Okay, now you have to have a place to tell them you are living, preferably nothing permanent."

"How about my pick-up truck and camper, we can tell them we are living out of that." Mac offered.

"Perfect, now other than the giant we ran into, there were no other carnies that I saw who would be able to take on either of you, so I don't think there will be any trouble." I knew Mac and Buck both being over six feet and very muscular would be able to whip the ass off of any of the men we saw. "But carnies can be viscous if cornered, from what I've heard. So tread lightly."

"I'm not worried, we'll get in and find out what's going on," Buck said confidently, giving me hope.

"Okay, you two get your act together and I'll give you directions to the site." We were finished for now and everyone left the room except Lacey and me.

"I'm sorry, I wasn't trying to give you a hard time about money," she said.

"Lacey you've worked for me for over a year and you've always kept everyone in line and put up with all the bull the guys threw at you, so you deserve a raise and you'll get one. So beginning Monday start yourself at double what you are making now, we have enough business to keep up. Does that work for you?"

She looked shocked at the offer and gave me a hug. "Thank you so much. Jessie is now getting

34

to the age where she needs things that she didn't need before. This will help with everything."

"Okay, get going and give Mac a good-bye kiss; he's running off to join the carnival."

She laughed and we went out to the lobby. Mac turned and said, "I'll run Lacey and Jessie home and come back with the camper." They left and Buck was on his cell phone explaining to Maria what he was going to be doing. He gave me a thumbs up and hung up.

An hour later Buck and Mac had the camper looking like two macho men were living out of it. We put in plenty of beer cans and tossed clothes around to give it a homey look. They were dressed in bluejeans and cutoff t-shirts with their muscles bulging, looking all the part. I gave them the directions to the carnival and who to see.

"Act like you're just needing a job for extra money and that you can travel. You both know how to bullshit, but if you get caught don't kill anyone unless it's absolutely necessary."

They got in the truck and drove off. Angelo, Penny and I stood with Earl and Paula watching them go.

"Think this is going to work?" Earl asked.

Dark Carnival Murders

"I'm hoping on it. Buck and Mac both look like bikers and rowdies, they shouldn't have any problems. Now if you and I went in for a job, they'd carry us out on a rail," I said smiling at him. "All we can do now is wait. I need to call the Walkers and let them to know they have to wait too. It's going to be a rough night for them." I went back to my office to call.

~~*~~

Mac drove into the carnival parking and up near the tent. It was late but the crowd was still at a busy level. Buck and Mac got out and wandered around the place to get familiar with the rides again, it had been a long time for both to have been away from that kind of work.

They spotted the huge trailer that held the office and went up the stairs to the door. Buck knocked and heard someone yell to come in, they entered. There was a small counter with a rather rough looking woman behind the grill that separated the entrance from the rest of the truck.

"Can I help you mugs?" the woman growled.

36

"We're looking for work," Buck growled back. The woman smiled, Buck had that effect on women, even the ugly ones.

"What kind of work?" she said nicer now.

"Carnie work, we've both got experience running the rides." Buck was trying to sound like a low life.

"What makes you think we need help?" she fired back.

"Carnivals always need help. You gain people, you lose people from quitters to those going to jail. We just figured maybe you had a couple holes to fill."

"Maybe we do, what are your backgrounds, criminal I mean?"

Buck grinned, he had a troubled youth and could prove it, "I've had a few run-ins with the law, back in Detroit, nothing near murder, mostly petty crimes, drunk driving, a few high speed chases. Never killed anyone I would admit to."

The woman looked to Mac, he smiled and said, "I was a choir boy in Kansas, maybe a few small infractions bending the law but I'm clean."

"No major warrants out for either of you? I will check, so don't bullshit me."

Buck said, giving her his famous walrus smile, "We be good boys now, ma'am."

She sat staring at them, then said, "You'll have to talk to Mr. Dark, the owner, but I'll put in a good word. We need two big guys like you, now days we can only seem to get scrawny druggies and burnouts. Hang on and I'll call him" She picked up a two way radio and called for the man. He came back to her and she told him that there were two men looking for work. "I think you need to take a look," she said with a smile.

Buck and Mac stood in the small lobby of the office and waited. Then the door flew open and in walked the strange man in the top hat. Buck could see what Jim had told him about how the man looked evil.

He strutted around Buck and Mac sizing them up like cattle. "I'm impressed, do you have any background in carnie work?"

Buck went over his resume of the Bob-Lo island work then Mac explained what his qualifications were. Dark just paced.

"Either of you into any criminal activities, anything that you wouldn't do if asked, if you know what I mean."

"If you mean would we be above doing something shady? Anything short of murder wouldn't bother us. If you know what I mean."

"Where are you from?" Dark asked Buck.

"Detroit, all around, I moved a lot."

Dark smiled and asked, "Did you know Piper Davis?"

Amazingly, Buck did, "Greasy little creep, into theft and kiddie porn, rode with the Vigilantes bike club. That Piper Davis?"

Dark smiled and told the woman, "Martha, get these men on the payroll. You two can start on the round-up. Can you handle that?"

"We'll have people stuck to the walls," Buck said with his grin.

"Just don't kill anyone... yet," Dark said with a smirk and went out of the trailer.

Buck smiled as the woman pulled the paperwork for them to fill out. They had to lie as to their addresses, luckily Buck still carried his Michigan driver's license and showed it to her. Mac just said Buck was driving their truck and he had his license taken away. She accepted that, Buck was sure she didn't really care.

They finished up and the woman called on the two way for some person named Skeeter to come to the office. About ten minutes later a man entered, he was introduced as Skeeter Lynn. He was about half the size of Buck and looked like he hadn't bathed in a few weeks.

"Yeah, Martha what's up?" he spoke with a toothless grin.

"Dark said to get these mugs started on the round-up. Watch them for a while to make sure everything is good."

"You got it sexy woman," he said with a cough. He led Buck and Mac to the midway and over to a corner where the massive ride sat. Its job was to spin fast, forcing people against the walls as it lifted them off the ground. It was centrifugal force that held the victims to the wall.

Skeeter set them up with the ride and watched for a bit. Luckily the round-up was a standard ride so Buck and Mac both had experience with it.

Skeeter smiled and said, "Yeah you know what you're doing. Have fun." He walked away as Buck pulled his cell phone to call Jim.

*

Chapter 5

I was in my office and picked up the desk phone and dialed the Walkers. The husband came on and asked right off if we found them.

"Mr. Walker, please be patient, we have two men now inside the carnival and they should be able to find out what happened, you just have to wait now. I'll keep you informed as soon as we have something. This is our first priority and I'm going to be bringing the police in shortly. We are doing our best."

He was silent, then, "I guess we will just have to depend on you, thank you and we'll be here." He hung up but I could tell he was upset, I didn't blame him, now I really had to find the boys. I went back out to the lobby and was standing behind the couch when my cell phone buzzed.

Dark Carnival Murders

I grabbed it from my pocket and read the caller ID, it was Buck. "Can you talk?" I asked.

I could hear a loud amount of noise and he yelled into the phone, "Yeah, we got the job, this Dark guy looks evil as you said. We just started, will fill you in later," he said and hung up.

I looked to the expectant group sitting in the lobby, "They're in." Everyone gave a sigh of relief and Earl said, "Now it's up to them."

"Yeah, but I'm going to call Lynn to let her know what we're up to and to be ready." It was just after five in the afternoon, I didn't know if Lynn was in the city or still on her honeymoon, I hated to interrupt if they were, but I called. She came on after three rings.

"Now what do you want?" she laughed.

"I wanted to see if your honeymoon is still going on or are you back to work?"

"Hell, we just got into the airport in LA and were just heading out to find our car. I hope you don't have a major crime to report?"

"No, just missing boys, two, ages ten and eight and we're suspicious of a carnival that rolled into town this week. Long story, I'll fill you in when you hit town, call me."

"Okay, we have a long ride back to Vegas so it will be later tonight or tomorrow, if it's not a priority."

"As of right now we have the situation sort of under control but will let you know more later. Enjoy your ride," I said and hung up.

"I hate waiting," I said and sat next to Penny on the couch. "Lynn and Deacon have a couple hours before they are settled back home. Buck and Mac probably won't find much on their first night, but I hope they do some snooping. We may as well go home; I'm worn out from running around in the heat today."

"And you missed your nap," Penny added.

I looked at my watch and said, "We could still snuggle when we get home."

"Forget it, you can't snuggle without fooling around," she snickered.

"Fine, let's just go home then."

Earl and Paula got up and said they were going to get something to eat and left. I asked

Dark Carnival Murders

Angelo how he enjoyed the day at the carnival.

"I liked it, well not the missing kids, but the whole thing was good. If you need any of my contacts in the family to help finding the boys just let me know."

I thought about bringing in Angelo's whole family and have them attack the carnival and put Dark in cement boots. Of course, Lynn would have a fit, so I may need what the mob could find out for me without murdering anyone. Penny gathered her things and the three of us went to the van.

We arrived home and I took Willy out from the kitchen to do his business, as Angelo went to his guesthouse. Penny was nuking a couple pasties and I settled on the couch. We ate our meal and then watched TV with our beer and chips.

Around eight, there was a loud knocking on our front door. I wondered why the alarms hadn't gone off then realized that I hadn't set them. I peeked through the little hole in the door and saw a big nose. Then I saw teeth, they were attached to Deacon. The goof ball was smiling in the peep hole, I opened the door and let them in.

"Should we be honored that you came right here from your honeymoon?" I asked.

"Don't flatter yourself, we went home and changed, then came here. Now what is this big case you have?" Lynn asked.

"Well, it may not have anything to do with you; it's a missing person case."

She shrugged, "I can handle it; we all share now since they've been cutting back on departments. Is it missing or a kidnapping?"

"Not sure, but the boys have been missing for a day now. If they might have just wandered off, but they should be back by now."

"Talk to me Sherlock," she said as she and Deacon sat.

I explained the whole day from the early morning tent departure to Buck and Mac getting a job.

"Carnie Buck, I love that. I need to go take pictures tomorrow," Lynn laughed.

"I'm sure he'd appreciate that. Now can you do anything?"

"Nope, not until we have probable cause or some evidence that the boys went there in the first place. No judge would sign a search warrant on conjecture. Now if Buck and Mac can find something that would allow us to go in and search. Of course, we could go in and ask nicely if we can look, and maybe they'll give us permission to look see, but I doubt it. From past experience, carnivals aren't too cooperative with us. In the morning I'll do a background check on this Jacob Dark, maybe he'll come up dirty and we can harass him."

"I thought about having Angelo bring in his family but I knew you'd never approve that."

"Damn skippy, I don't want to see any wiseguys near this. Or just don't let me see them." She grinned and asked, "We've been here for twenty minutes and still haven't been offered a celebratory wedding drink, are you getting cheap as well as senile?"

"Are you able to drink being pregnant?" Penny asked.

"In moderation and small amounts, it's still early in the term and I don't drink much."

I went to the kitchen and opened the brandy we had for special occasions. I poured the liquor into four glasses and put them on a tray. I handed out the glasses and sat.

I held up my glass, "Here's to a long and

happy marriage and a happy baby." We drank, Lynn sipped.

Deacon told us all the details of their honeymoon in Hawaii and left not much out, much to Lynn's dismay. She had to hit him a few times.

We sat talking for a while and then they said they were tired from their trip back and we finished up the evening.

At the door Lynn said, "I'll get on this in the morning. I can understand what the parents are going through, especially now that I'm going to have a child myself."

"I'll be in touch," I said. They left and I set the alarms and pulled Penny to the bedroom. She was dragging, but short of carrying her, I got her to bed.

~~*~~

Around midnight, Buck and Mac had finished the shift of getting people on and off the round-up. The crowd had thinned and then finally went home. Buck and Mac closed down the ride and secured it, then they turned to see Mr. Dark approach.

"Men, I watched you both and you attracted a lot of nice young ladies to this ride. Women like big strong men like you, I think you can be handy. Are you open to making a lot more money?"

"We don't have to kill anyone, do we?" Buck said with a grin.

"Oh goodness no, just convince a few nice ladies to join our traveling show, that's all. Not hard is it?" Dark said with an evil smile.

Buck leaned towards Dark and said, "I get what you are saying, we don't really need to convince them do we?"

"You understand, fantastic, we have a deal?"

"As long as the money is good too."

"Oh, it can be if you deliver the goods."

"We can do the job," Buck grinned.

"Fantastic, you can go off to your little camper for now, but I think maybe we can arrange better quarters for you. Oh and I called my friend Piper Davis and he remembers you too. He said to say hi and gave a glowing report of your past, I like it." He turned and walked away. Buck looked to Mac and smiled.

Bob Moats

~~*~~

The next morning, Sunday, Angelo was preparing his famous sausage, eggs and cheese biscuit sandwiches and the smell pulled me from my sleep. I hit the bathroom and quickly went to the kitchen before Penny ate everything.

I had my fill since Angelo made extras and even Willy had his treat. Penny was making a piggy out of herself and I joked to her that her butt was getting bigger. Big mistake.

She finished her sandwich, stuck her tongue out at me and stalked off to her bathroom.

"Mr. R., I think you may be in trouble, women don't like being told their asses look fat," Angelo said.

"Angelo, you are wise beyond your age. I knew as soon as it slipped out of my mouth. The thing about Penny is that she holds it in until the right moment then she lets loose. So I'm in terror all day," I said with a laugh.

I finished up my meal and then my cell phone buzzed, it was Buck. "Talk to me," I said.

"I think we got him," was all he said and hung up.

*

Chapter 6

I figured Buck was in the middle of something or he would have said more, so I just had to wait, but the news was encouraging. Penny came back out from the bathroom, all dressed and ready for the day. I wondered if my fat ass comment had settled.

She kissed my cheek and pinched my butt. "Hmm… getting a bit cheeky there, lard ass."

I just had to hold in the laugh and hope that was it. Then she said, "Angelo we need to get Mr. R. a bigger stool so his butt can fit on it." Angelo held his laugh also.

Penny leaned down to pick up Willy and said to him, "Be careful baby, so daddy doesn't sit on you."

"Okay! I apologize for my insensitive remark, can we drop it now," I pleaded.

"All right blubber butt, it's over." She kissed me again and took Willy out the sliding patio door to the backyard.

I just shook my head and Angelo laughed aloud. I stood and went through the patio door to the back and found Penny standing on the lawn with Willy running around the yard like a mad dog.

"He's getting his exercise, we need to make him walk more instead of carrying him all the time," she said.

"I agree, but he's so small he's liable to get stepped on," I said just as my cell phone buzzed. I pulled it out and the caller ID said it was Deacon. "Hey big guy, is the honeymoon over yet?" I said.

"Not yet, we are just getting started. Just called to see if you're going to that carnival again. Lynn did a quick check and could find nothing on Jacob Dark. She has Warren checking on the city permits for the carnival to set up and see what that says. Otherwise, he's not on the radar, no criminal past that she can find. Heard from Buck yet?"

"As a matter of fact, he called about ten minutes ago and cryptically said that we got him and hung up. I suppose we'll have to wait until he can talk. Are you and Lynn thinking about going to the carnival?"

"If you guys are, Lynn wants to see carnie Buck as she's calling him now."

I turned to Penny and quickly told her what Deacon said, she replied, "I'm all for going to see carnie Buck too."

"Okay, tell Lynn that you guys can meet us at my office in an hour. Bring a couple of fans," I said and hung up.

"Willy can go with us this time, he may enjoy the kiddie boat ride," Penny said with a grin and called to Willy. He came running and she picked him up and headed back into the house. Angelo was just finishing cleaning the kitchen and I asked if he'd like to go to the carnival again.

"Thanks Mr. R. but I got plans for today and I'm calling mom this afternoon, she may come out for a visit."

Penny heard this and made a little happy squeal, "When do you think she may be here?"

"We have to work it out, I'll let you know. You have to recommend some good shows to go to also. Mom is going to be here for at least five days so we need to have things to do."

"Is Gino coming also?" I asked.

"It's not common knowledge whether he is coming or not, you get what I mean," he said with a wink.

I wasn't going to ask further, it sounded like a clandestine trip, one mob capo getting out of town under cover. I hope there was going to be no criminal activities that the Feds may spoil Angelo seeing his mother.

"Don't worry, Mr. R. it's all good, Gino just needs to get away from the life every so often."

"Good, you know that they are more than welcome to visit us while they are here. Are you putting them up in the Tropicana again?"

"Yeah, mom likes the place so it's going to be where they will stay."

Penny spoke, "You make sure that Francis and I can have a day to ourselves, just the women."

"I think she is already planning on it, she asked me to get reservations for that spa she enjoyed last time she was here, and she said to get one for you too."

Penny grinned, "Great, I'll look forward to it."

"We have to get moving if we are going to meet Deacon and Lynn," I interrupted. "Angelo, the house is yours if you need it."

"Thanks Mr. R. but I'm going to be gone most the day."

I didn't ask what he was up to, and really didn't want to know, especially if it involved his mob friends. The less I knew the better. Penny went to get her things and Willy's leash.

"Not bringing the carry bag?" I asked.

"Throw it in the van in case," she said.

We went outside to the van, drove to the office and saw Deacon's huge pick-up in front of the building. I was hoping that Lynn didn't have any ideas about going shopping at the mall. We parked and they came over. Lynn had a camera hanging around her neck.

"You were serious about taking carnie Buck's picture," I said.

"Bet your bippy, I want this to show Maria and Trapper," she said. "Speaking of him, where is he?"

"I haven't spoke to him since Friday when he told me he and Samantha were going to try and see if they can rekindle their relationship," I said.

"So Trapper's horny and Sam is available," Deacon laughed.

"Probably, but that's his business. Now shall we hit the desert before it gets too hot out?" I said.

We all got into my van and I drove back south to the carnival. Parking wasn't so bad this time and we weren't too far away from the midway. We entered and went down the first row of rides, until we got to the corner where I spotted Buck and Mac at the entrance to the round-up. Buck was operating the controls and Mac was helping people on and off the massive ride.

Lynn spotted them also and we headed there. I said that we didn't want to give away their cover, so I told the women to just act like they were interested in Buck and Mac, since I could see there were a few women crowding around them. Penny handed Willy to me as Deacon and I stood back while she and Lynn went up to the metal railing surrounding the ride. They stood near the entrance where the now sweating men herded the people onto the ride.

Buck saw Lynn and Penny, he didn't make a fuss but after the people were on the ride, Mac closed the door and stood back as Buck started the thing running. The huge round machine started to spin forcing the people standing against the wall to be pinned. The whole thing started to lift off the ground, giving the riders the feeling they were going to fall, but wouldn't.

Lynn moved up to Buck while still watching the ride spin, she glanced over and smiled to Mac and Buck. Buck wiped the sweat from his head and moved closer to the women.

"I got some goods on Dark," he said quietly, "He asked Mac and me to help induce women into joining the carnival if you know what I mean." He went over and pushed a few controls to take the ride higher. The people were all screaming, then he started to bring the ride back down.

Lynn leaned to Penny and said, "So Dark wants to kidnap a few women for possible human trafficking, but we need to find the boys first."

Buck brought the ride back down and slowed the spin. After it stopped, Mac helped people off the ride. More people crowded the gate to get on, covering Lynn and Penny from unwanted eyes. As Mac herded the people, Buck leaned against the fence and spoke again.

"Dark wants to talk to us tonight more about what he'd like us to do. So far we haven't found anything about the missing boys, no chatter from the other men. We're going to keep our ears and eyes open, so be patient. Once Dark has us do anything illegal, I'll call you in. I don't want to get involved in kidnapping, so don't forget that we are undercover."

Lynn smiled and said, "Don't worry, you'll be covered, short of murder. I need to look into Dark's background too, and see if there have been any other complaints or activity that he may be involved in. Just do your best and keep me informed."

"I'll do that, now either ride or move away before they get suspicious." He stepped back to the controls as Lynn brought up her camera and snapped off a couple pictures of him and Mac.

"Lacey will love this," she said to Penny as they moved away from the ride.

They came back to us and Lynn passed the info she got from Buck. "I hope the boys are still alive, but I believe they are, it's got to be a human trafficking operation. They move from town to town and grab a few people, not enough to draw attention, then move on. A carnival is a perfect operation."

"I hope that's going to comfort the Walkers, that their boys are probably still alive. I just hope they haven't been shipped off to some foreign country to be slaves. That's not good."

*

Chapter 7

We walked around until I finally saw Jacob Dark and pointed him out to Lynn. She brought her camera up and was pretending to take a few pictures of the rides, then snapped a couple of Dark as he was talking to a well-dressed dark skinned man in his late fifties. Lynn brought her camera down and said, "Rather ominous looking isn't he?"

"Yep, he's dressing for the part. He's a rather pleasant speaking person but it's mostly for show I presume. Buck didn't say much about him?"

"He didn't say much about anything other than being asked to grab off a few women. This carnival is here until Wednesday, so we only have three more days to shut down whatever Dark is doing," Lynn said.

"It's been over twenty-four hours since the boys disappeared. I hope Dark hasn't had enough time to take them anywhere. I also hope Buck and Mac can find something. Time will tell," I said as my cell phone buzzed. Caller ID said unknown, I answered, it was Mr. Walker. I told Penny, then I went off the side of the midway where I had a little privacy.

"Mr. Richards, have you found them yet?" he asked sounding a wreck.

"Mr. Walker, I'm at the carnival right now with a police detective friend of mine, I have two men working undercover to find them, please be patient. We are doing the best we can right now, but this is real life and crimes don't get solved in an hour like on TV." I was a bit harsh on him but he needed the reality check.

He was quiet for a beat then said, "I'll have to trust you, but we are both going crazy here. I don't know how to calm my wife; she's been pacing and driving me crazy also. I'm sorry I bothered you."

"You didn't bother me, if you hadn't called I might have thought you didn't care."

"Nonsense! We care deeply, we care so much it hurts to have to wait."

"I fully understand, I have a son also and I know how I'd feel if he disappeared."

"Do you have any idea what may have happened?"

I had an idea but didn't want to panic him, "We believe the boys are still alive, from what we have found out so far, but we just need to find their location. Now try and relax, I know it's a dumb thing to say, but I don't have any better words."

"Thank you Mr. Richards, we'll trust you, call as soon as you have something."

"I'll call even if we don't, just hang in, we'll talk later." I hung up and felt really bad, damn Dark and his people.

I went back to Penny and she asked if everything was all right, I said no, but stable for now.

We went one more time around the midway and then over to the tent where they had the sideshow. We paid the admission, went in and followed the narrow aisle to walk along the row of stages with all the geeks performing their talents.

We saw the rubber man who could twist himself into any small box or suitcase, which was handy if you wanted to be carry-on luggage on a plane. Then we watched the man who Earl and I watched sticking needles in his skin. I looked back for the giant but he wasn't there. We saw a good number of acts, the bearded lady, the man who could eat glass or any other horrible thing. My stomach was turning by the time we reached the exit.

Lynn said, "I've seen worse in my career as a cop."

"Including the wolf boy?" I asked.

"Every full moon," she said with a laugh.

Lynn's cell phone rang and she answered it, listened and then hung up. "Seems the permits to set up this festival were signed by a Lucius Cole, representing the carnival. Ever heard of him?"

"No, did Warren dig a little deeper?" I asked.

"He said he's going to check on him shortly and let me know."

"While we wait, I'm getting hungry. What say we go eat," I said.

"Sure, but no fast food, I want real food." Penny said.

"Bistros?" I said.

Everyone agreed and we headed back towards the van. As we got close to the trailer that housed the carnival office, I said to hold on.

"What's on your devious little mind, and I do mean little?" Lynn asked.

"Wait here, Deacon come with me," I said as I went to the trailer, Deacon in tow. I went up the stairs and into the lobby of the office. A grouchy looking woman was sitting behind the grillwork.

"Can I help you two," she growled.

"May I speak to Lucius Cole," I said simply.

The woman just stared, not speaking. "Where do you know this Mr. Cole from?"

"I don't, but his name is on the city permits he signed for the carnival. We're just checking his validity."

"What authority do you have?"

Deacon pulled his badge and flashed it. "Now can we see Mr. Cole?"

"He's not in Las Vegas, his office is in Florida. He came into town and took care of the paperwork and went back home. Sorry, but if you'll leave your card I'll have him get in touch with you."

"I was under the impression that Mr. Dark owned the carnival."

"He does, but he has investors and Mr. Cole holds the position of CEO. Now if you can leave your card."

I said, "That won't be necessary, we just wanted to verify he existed. Thank you," I said and we left.

Back with the women I said, "The mysterious Mr. Cole isn't in the state, he's supposedly in Florida. And he is the CEO of Dark carnival. This is far reaching."

"Well hopefully Warren can find something about Cole. Now let's go eat."

We got back to the van and drove out to go to

Bistros where we dined. It was now almost five and not much had been accomplished. I felt bad that I didn't have any good news to tell the Walkers.

As we sat at the table, Lynn got a call and after she took it she said to us, "Trouble, we have two more parents reporting that their children didn't come home from the carnival when they said they would. Dark is either taking more than he needs or something more sinister is going on. Warren has one set of the parents at the precinct. Maybe we should go talk to them?"

We paid the bill and I drove them to their truck, waited for them to head out and followed. We arrived at LVMPD a few minutes later and parked. Warren had a man and woman in Lynn's office at her request and Penny, Deacon and I stood just inside the doorway as Lynn sat at her desk.

"Hello, I'm Lieutenant Lynn Carter, and you are?"

The man spoke, "We're Joan and Harry Felton, our son Jeff told us he was going to the carnival this morning with some friends, he said he'd be home by two because we had family coming over. He never came back. I called his friend Steve and he said Jeff split off from them at the carnival and then they couldn't find him. I've called his cell but he's not answering, this is not

64

like him, he's a good kid."

"Do you have a picture of him?"

"Yes, the other detective asked us to bring one," he said as he pulled out a wallet size photo and handed it to Lynn.

"You know we don't usually investigate missing persons for at least 48 hours, but sometimes the circumstances warrant a look." She didn't want to mention the two missing boys yet. "If he should return, call me." She handed him her business card and he put it in his shirt pocket. "Sometimes things just get screwed up and he may be off doing something boys don't tell their parents about. Does he have a girlfriend?"

The wife spoke now, "He's popular, he has a few that follow him around, maybe he's off with one of them, but he wouldn't miss our family get-together. He said he'd be back."

"Okay, it's no good sitting here guessing, but we'll do what we can. Now just go home in case he returns and call if he does." Lynn stood and the Feltons followed her out as we stood aside from the door. Lynn took them to the entrance and then came back.

"Could be nothing, or could be Dark is getting careless and grabbing more," she said as she came into the office.

Warren appeared at the door and said, "Lynn, the other parents just called and their daughter has returned home, so she's safe."

"Good, one less to worry about. Thanks Greg." Warren left and we all sat. "I think I'll use this to send a few uniforms into the carnival with copies of the boy's picture and ask around. It may stir up something and Dark may make a move, so Buck can observe what's going on. Buck said Dark wanted to talk to him and Mac later tonight about the deal he has going. We need to find the location of the boys and get them out."

Warren was back at the door with a folder, "Lynn, here's all I could find on Lucius Cole, he's out of Gibsonton, Florida and has no priors, but he is being watched by the Feds for possible drug trafficking and gun running. When I made my inquiry, it brought a flag up in the FBI database and I got a call from some agent out of Florida and he asked why we wanted to know. His contact number is in the folder."

"Thanks again Greg." Lynn dialed the number in the folder and got an agent Bill Kestor. She explained who she was and why we were inquiring about Lucius Cole. She listened for a couple minutes and then told him all we had so far. She finished and hung up.

"He doesn't know anything about human trafficking, so he asked us to keep on top of it. He also told me Dark is dangerous and to be careful."

*

Chapter 8

Lynn yelled for Warren and he came running, "Can you somehow get an itinerary of where Dark's carnival has been and see what you can find about missing persons in the areas."

"You got it," he said and went off.

"So he's traveling the country and kidnapping people for what? Human trafficking? Where are they sending the people?" I asked.

"Most of the trafficking involves foreign countries, Arab countries, Russian, even England. The rich don't care, they just want slaves or playthings to rape when they feel the need. It's nothing new and hard to stop."

I said, "I remember back when Buck, Earl and I traveled to New York to find the girl taken by human traffickers. The girl was Angelo's cousin's girlfriend. Luckily, we found her before they totally ruined her, holding her as a prostitute in a club out there. But what do they want with young boys?"

"You really need to ask? There are so many perverts out there, it's doesn't surprise me at all. All ages including men, young and old, are taken each year. If this carnival is behind this, I want them to be taken down," Lynn said with a definite hatred in her voice.

~~*~~

Buck and Mac were going on a break to chow down in the carnies' tent behind the office trailer. The men were all sitting around chattering about the day and then Buck and Mac came in and sat at a long table with a couple of them.

"So where is the show going to after here?" Buck asked to start a conversation.

The men went silent and gave Buck a hard stare.

One man finally spoke, "I hear Dark is looking for a new Chester."

Buck's jaw tightened, he knew the term, "Why, did you lose the job as child molester?"

The man straightened up and started to stand, Skeeter Lynn stood from another table and told the man to chill, the man looked to Skeeter and sat back down.

Skeeter came to the middle of the tent and shouted to everyone, "Listen up, these two ride jockeys are in good standing with Dark, and you know you don't want his grief. They aren't forty milers, they have background. Buck here is a friend of Piper's and you know what that means. So show some respect."

The rest of the men loosened up and greeted Buck and Mac. "You really rode with the Vigilantes?" one man asked.

Buck grinned and said, "I was acquainted with them, I was a loaner, had a Harley 94 Ultra Classic, Shriner Edition. We just need the work and Mac and I are both carnies at heart, so *MISTER* Dark took us on." Buck gave a heavy emphasis on the mister.

Skeeter spoke, "You two are to meet with *MISTER* Dark at midnight in the office, after we drop the awnings. He wants to set you up with his pet project. Now enjoy your meal and get back to the dog house, the clems await."

Buck and Mac finished their meals in relative silence then went back to the round-up.

~~*~~

Lynn was briefing the four uniforms who she was sending to the carnival to search for the missing teen. "Just go around, being obvious and ask questions, show the pictures and see what you can stir up."

I was standing nearby and said, "Lynn, why don't you have them take the picture of the other two boys and have them shown? It may stir up more than showing one boy."

"Good idea, give me the picture and I'll make copies." She turned back to the men, "Now be careful, Jim has two men working undercover, and we don't want to queer their job." She looked to Tim and said, "You know Buck and Mac, they're both working a ride called the round-up, so point them out to your men, but don't give away their cover." Tim agreed.

One of the officers asked, "Lieutenant, if there are two men undercover, why are we going in?"

"I can tell you're new, right?" The officer nodded. "Well, we want the bad guys to get nervous and maybe screw up. Buck and Mac are watching and will let us know what they are doing. Understand?"

He nodded again, and Lynn went to make copies of the photo. Shortly after the officers went off to do their search; Lynn and I went back to her office where Penny and Deacon were relaxing at Lynn's desk, we sat.

"I'm hoping Buck calls us after he gets briefed by Dark. All we can do is wait until after midnight," I said.

"So are you going to stay here while we wait?" Lynn asked.

"Oh hell no, I'm taking my beautiful wife home and I'll call you when I hear from my spies." I looked to Penny and said, "Shall we go get something to eat then go relax at home?"

Penny expressed her agreement and we said our good-byes and left. We drove out after we agreed on a place to eat, so we went to Arturo's and had a nice sit down meal. We were back home and I let Willy out to do his business.

"Hey Mr. R. I thought I heard you guys pull in," Angelo said over the side fence, startling me.

"Hey Angelo, how's your day going? Did you accomplish everything you set out to do?"

"Yep, had a nice visit with some new friends and then I talked to my mother. Is Mrs. R. in the house?"

"Sure Angelo, go on in, she was in the kitchen last I saw her."

"Thanks," he said and went to the patio door and called in. I heard Penny yell to come in and he vanished through the opening. Willy had finished his business and I cleaned up after him then we went back in. Angelo and Penny were in the living room sitting on the couch talking. I plopped down next to Penny and listened to their conversation.

"She said she'd call you as soon as she got in town," Angelo was saying.

Penny turned to me and said, "Francis is

going to be here Tuesday for five days then go back to New York. Gino is coming also, but that's not for public knowledge. So you and the head of the Traviano mob family can go do men things," she said with a grin.

"What, target practice? Angelo, is Gino coming out for business or pleasure?" I asked.

"A little of both, he has business but it won't take long, then he is going to relax around the pool of the Tropicana."

I figured it wouldn't take long to whack someone, then relax. Penny spoke, "Tell Gino he can come and relax around our pool."

"I'll tell him but he likes the scenery around the public pools. More bikinis to watch," Angelo said with a sly smile.

"Now that I can agree on," I said.

"Don't agree too hard, I still look good in a bikini."

I better agree or lose my head, "Yes babe, you still got it."

We sat relaxing with our beer and TV then Angelo went off to his little home as Penny and I waited for some news from Buck.

~~*~~

Around midnight the carnival had started to close up, Skeeter came to Buck and said that Dark wanted them. Buck and Mac followed Skeeter to the office and they went in. Dark was in a small office in the back of the trailer and welcomed them. Skeeter left and the two men sat before Dark.

"Glad you agreed to help with my little venture. I'm going by what Piper told me about your background, and I'm trusting your word on Mac. Are either of you against a little criminal activities?"

"Anything but murder, we're open for," Buck answered.

"No nothing like that, I'm in the life business. I have certain clients who need people to work for them and they have special needs for who they are. Many of my clients need women and occasionally young men of certain ages and ethnicities to work for them."

Buck smiled and said, "Cutting to the chase, we're talking about human trafficking aren't we?"

Dark grinned his evil smirk and said, "Yes, you do understand. Have you ever been involved in this?"

"I got into a little of it out in New York, I was involved with a company called Rex Erotica. They were grabbing strippers from Detroit."

Dark perked up and said, "Ah yes, I've heard about that, messy business and untimely end for the owners."

"I was on the fringes between Detroit and New York, transporting the strippers, so I never got caught. Now let's get to it, what do you want Mac and me to do?"

"The both of you are very good looking and masculine. I've watched and could see you attract a number of very nice looking ladies. All you have to do is get them talking, flirt a little then invite them to an after-hours party that I will be having at the Luxor Hotel. Once you have them there, I have people who will take care of the rest. Simple enough and it will earn you a little extra in your draw pay."

"Sounds good to me, are you in?" Buck looked to Mac.

"I'm fine with it," Mac said quietly.

"Okay you start tomorrow, it's better to pull them in later, after dark when the best come out, and less time for them to change their minds."

"Do you need a certain number of bodies?" Buck asked.

"Well, no more than four good ones. Let's not make it too difficult. So go get some beauty sleep, tomorrow we start."

*

Chapter 9

It was almost twelve-thirty when my cell phone buzzed, I saw by the caller ID that it was Buck. I answered, "Hey, what's happening?"

"Dark is a bastard. He wants Mac and me to lure four women into a party at the Luxor where someone will kidnap them and put them into slavery. I don't have the details as to where they go, but hopefully tomorrow I'll have more for you. Tim and his cop buddies came by and asked Mac and me a few questions about the missing boys, they did good to not give us away. Tim said they scoured the whole place and found no one that had any answers."

"Of course not; they wouldn't give anything away to the cops. I'll call Lynn and maybe we can figure out something to keep the women you attract safe from harm. Are you able to take calls again tonight?"

"Yeah, Mac and I are in his camper, so it's safe to take calls. I'll be awake for a while and wait to hear from you."

"Okay, hang in and I'll get back to you." I hung up and dialed Lynn, she came on after two rings.

"What do you have for me?" she said without saying hello.

"Buck said that he and Mac are to lure four women into a party tomorrow night at the Luxor where they will be kidnapped for transport to who knows where. He'll try and give me a few more details when he gets them. I have an idea if you can work it out?"

"Talk to me, I'm always interested in your ideas. It usually saves me from thinking," she said with a laugh.

"Can you have Deacon see if they have some undercover female officers in vice that could pose as Buck's guests to this party? Maybe wire them and have your men waiting to follow where ever they take them."

"I got it, yes that could work. I'll tell Deacon and have him arrange it. Tell Buck the plan and I'll arrange for the women to give Buck a signal as to who they are."

"Get it set up and get back to me. I'll pass it on to Buck."

Lynn said she would and we hung up. I called Buck back and told him my idea, he liked it. "I'll call you again with whatever Lynn can come up with," I said.

We finished the call and I put my head back on the couch.

"Hey, you can't rest, there are children out there missing and you have to find them," Penny said.

"Babe, if Buck and Mac haven't found them

78

yet, I don't think I could tonight. We have a lead now and hopefully it will pan out to finding where they are taking the boys. But it won't happen until tomorrow, so we need to get some rest now."

"All right, but don't get too lazy on this. Now I'm going to bed, you can join me, but for sleep only." She stood and went off to the bedroom, leaving me thinking about the activities of the last couple days. I hated it when my mind wandered and I wanted to sleep. It wasn't a good combination.

I stood and let my body fall into place since I had been on the couch for the last five hours. I followed my wife to the bedroom and found her in bed already, asleep. She was fast on her feet and fast in bed.

I undressed quietly and slid under the new satin sheets we bought. They felt cool and slippery on my weary body, I relaxed. I lay there thinking back to when Buck, Earl and I had gone on a mission to track down the trafficking of strippers from Detroit to New York. Rex Erotica had an office in the north of Detroit and the women they grabbed where chained and held captive until the runners could transport them to the whorehouses of New York where they were forced to prostitute themselves. The office where they were held captive was disgusting and the women were treated badly. We rescued Angelo's cousin's girlfriend from the human trafficking machine and shut them down. Unfortunately, I took a bullet on that adventure and almost died, but Penny and the Traviano mob family stood by me as I recovered. Say what you will about mob families, they are concerned about their friends.

It didn't take long for me to pass out, I was asleep before the sun came up. When it did, my cell phone buzzed and it was Lynn.

"Just couldn't wait to wake me," I said as I looked to the digital clock on my bed stand, it read six-thirty.

"And miss a chance to get you up? I wanted to call an hour ago, but Deacon stopped me. I got some info for you to pass on to Buck," she said.

I came a little more awake on that note. I rolled over and saw Penny heading to her bathroom and turned my head to see Willy staring at me from where Penny was last sleeping. The dog licked my nose quickly, I pulled back and asked, "Did Deacon find a couple undercover officers to go to Dark's party?"

"Oh, yes he did. After it came out why we needed the undercover, we had more than enough volunteers to go to the carnival and get set up. I can send out six female officers to the party if that's enough?"

"Buck told me they only needed four, so go with that. We can make it a total cop party; that should scare up a few bad guys."

"Yes, but we don't want Dark to know his plan went south, we need to play it cautiously to get the whole picture as to where they are taking the women."

"Agreed, and I hope it is the same place they are taking the boys. We need to set up a phrase to let Buck know they are the undercover cops."

"How about, 'Hi Buck, Jim sent us'?"

"That's a bit obvious, how about 'We're here to party, Buck'?"

"I guess that could work, we just need to be sure everyone is on the same page."

"Buck knows how to keep the page the same. I'll call him and get his end set up. Are you going to check out the Luxor and see if there's anyone renting a room for a night?"

"Already got Warren on it. He'll find the room and we will have the rooms on either side covered. This is going to be fun."

"Just don't shoot up the Luxor, I'd hate to see your people get kicked out for excessive partying. You're not a rock band you know."

"Yea, well, we are going to be putting on a rock show tonight so just let Buck in on the plan. I'll call later with further details," she said then hung up.

Penny came out of her bathroom and jumped back into bed, snuggling up close. I said, "You had your chance last night, but you were too tired. So snuggle all you want, I'm not in the mood."

She carefully put her hand where it would start something, "You are evil," I said.

An hour later we were up and dressed, I was pulling my phone to call Buck. He came on after two rings, "Hey big guy, can you talk?"

"Yep, we're still in the camper and just getting ready to go out. What do you have?"

"Lynn and Deacon have four female undercover cops from Vice who will be approaching you and saying 'We're here to party, Buck'. That's your key to know it's them, try not to get too many other women involved."

"Will they be wired?"

"I didn't ask and Lynn didn't say, but I'm sure at least one will. They have to keep track of what's going on. Lynn said they are going to try and find which room they will be in and have it surrounded by cops on both sides. You're sure Dark said the Luxor?"

"That's what he said. If it suddenly changes I'll call."

"I hope it doesn't change now, there will be too many operations set up. But if it does, let me know."

"Will do, I have to go to work now, talk later." Buck hung up and I put my phone back in my pocket.

Penny was in the kitchen with Angelo whipping up a batch of pancakes, I didn't complain.

"Angelo, can you do some snooping for me and see what you can come up with on a carnival owned by Jacob Dark, with a CEO named Lucius Cole from Gibsonton, Florida?" I asked.

"Gibsonton, that's the carnival city isn't it?"

Angelo asked as he wrote the information on a pad of paper on the kitchen counter.

"As I understand it is. We don't have much on Cole yet, Dark is another matter, they don't have much on him at all."

"I'll get what I can. There's a gang of gypsies I know that are a tight knit mob family, they run shady sideshow games and fleece customers. I'll check on it with them."

"Good, thanks. Call me as soon as you get anything." I turned to Penny and said, "I should go call the Walkers and let them know we are still on the case."

"Just don't give them too much hope, this may not go like you hope it does," she said licking her syrupy fingers.

"You're just a ball of sunshine. Eat your grub and I'll take care of the Walkers." I left the kitchen and went to my home office and sat. I didn't really want to make the call, Penny was right, this may go bad.

*

Chapter 10

Jacob Dark entered the high end jewelry store on a hallway corner inside the Boulevard Mall on Maryland Boulevard just north of Flamingo Road. He wasn't wearing his top hat and was dressed conservatively in a dark suit, so the attractive brunette behind the counter gave the handsome man a broad smile and asked if she could help him.

"I'm looking for a necklace for my sister in Florida. Something in gold with a good number of diamonds and jade if that's possible," he spoke smoothly as he leaned closer to the woman over the counter.

She grinned, "I think I may be able to help with that." She went to another counter followed by Dark as she unlocked the back door of the cabinet, reaching in to retrieve a necklace that fit near to Dark's specifications. "I hope this is close to what you are looking for?"

"Ah, yes. This is very nice." He glimpsed at the price tag, "Well, this is certainly not cheap is it?"

The clerk smiled and said, "All our jewels are real and, yes, expensive. We cater to the Vegas tourists and locals who can afford the luxury of good jewelry. I could find a less expensive necklace for you, if you wish. We have some in the back in a special case with affordable prices."

"As much as I love my sister, I am not a rich man, please show me the special case then." Dark handed the necklace back to the clerk.

She locked the piece back in the cabinet and went off. Dark stood looking around the sales floor, there were two others looking at rings, probably wedding rings. He studied the overhead cameras around the room and then mentally noted the layout of the room. Before the sales clerk came back Dark was gone. She was slightly surprised, but figured the man didn't have that much to spend and probably would end up at Macy's jewelry department. It wasn't unusual for a customer to bolt at their prices.

~~*~~

I had arrived in my office building after seeing Penny off to her job, if you could call it a job. Sitting, talking to celebrities and getting a nice paycheck for it all, hardly a job. Now I had a job, I had to work hard to crack cases and face danger at every turn. Saving the city from horrible catastrophes such as dirty bombs and virus attacks, yes, I had a real job. Of course, I let Lynn and Deacon do most of the leg work, I just gave them the directions.

I liked my job, it paid well when I charged people, but I usually gave into pro bono work, since it helped people to get on with their lives. Even if I didn't get paid for it. I didn't care; I had a good deal of money from my book sales which were selling quite well and the few cases that we did charge for helped. Buck's security guard service made up for the biggest portion of our income; it was actually a small goldmine for what we charged.

I came in the back door yelling that I had arrived. Lacey was a great receptionist, bookkeeper, secretary and girl Friday, but she was a nervous one. I frequently startled her by my entering the lobby without announcing I was in the building. One day she would either have a heart attack or shoot me. I preferred the heart attack.

"Well, you do still work here," she said with a grin as I entered the inner lobby and up to the wall of a counter that kept the crazy clients away from her.

"Have I been away that long?"

"It seems like you breeze in to scare me and then go off to save the world. Now I'm without a husband because you sent him to join the carnival."

"He's doing good, he and Buck are going to kidnap a few women to put into slavery. Mac is working hard."

Lacey just stared at me, "Is that what he's going to do? Is he going to be arrested for it? Jessie doesn't need a criminal father."

"Don't worry, he's going to be safe and the women are going to be undercover police women, so all is good."

"You are devious," was all she said and went back to her paperwork, I went to my office and sat. I was startled when Earl came flying into my room and plopped down on the client chair.

"Okay, fill me in, what's happening?"

"Good morning to you too, all is well so far on the carnival case. Buck and Mac are expected to lure four women into slavery and we have a sting in place." I explained what had happened since I last saw Earl and he was nodding like a bobble head doll.

"There's nothing we can do now but wait and

hope the undercover cops will find something. Buck and Mac will need to be on their toes to pull this off. I hope the bad guys aren't too bright or suspicious to check the women too closely," I said.

"I'm sure it will go well from what you told me. There will be plenty of back-up, I'm sure Lynn wouldn't let anyone get hurt," Earl said as he stood. "I'll be around to help, call me when the plan starts. I love a good black ops covert action." He smiled and went out of the room.

I just sat back and looked around my office, I needed to redecorate.

~~*~~

Buck was sweating under the hot Vegas sun; he had to wipe the salty drips from his eyes frequently with the damp cloth he kept in a can of cool water sitting by the control panel. Mac was busy running back and forth escorting people to the huge machine. Buck leaned against a pole of the cage where the controls were when he heard a voice to his left.

"Hey big guy, do you party?" said the voice

from an attractive brunette. She was barely twenty and had on a tube top that held back her enormous breasts. Buck could tell right away she wasn't a cop.

"Sorry babe, I don't do customers. Try the sideshow." Buck grinned and started up the machine. The woman gave him a frown and walked away.

About an hour later two women came up and said the phrase Buck was waiting to hear.

"I may have a party you might like, it's at the Luxor. Just a few good people who like to have a good time, if you're interested?" Buck said to them.

The blonde smiled and said, "Can I bring a couple friends?"

"Sure but only four is the limit. Can you handle that?"

"I can, when shall we meet you and where?"

"Eleven-thirty, right here. And dress to party."

The two women laughed and went off. Buck was ready to take a break so he called Skeeter Lynn to cover for him and Mac. About ten minutes later, Skeeter and another man came up and filled in as Buck and Mac went off to the tent to eat. On the way Buck stopped in front of a porta-potty and told Mac he had to take a pee. Buck entered the commode, locked the door and pulled his cell phone.

~~*~~

I was in the lobby talking to Lacey about Jessie and how she was doing in school when my cell phone buzzed, it was Buck.

"Hey Buck, what's the word?" I asked.

"Not a lot, I'm in the potty, I just made contact with the women, told them to meet us at our ride at eleven-thirty. Have everyone ready to go." He hung up and I dialed Lynn.

"Just talked to Buck, he's made contact with the officers, so all is good to go," I said when Lynn answered.

"Warren found the room where they may be, it's a good bet since the room was rented to a

91

Lucius Cole. He's either in town or they are just using his name."

"I thought hotels need identification to register now?"

"Easy enough to fake, especially if they do this enough times. Anyway, we have both rooms on either side registered to LVMPD. We have one woman wired, not taking chances, but I don't think the men will be worried that they are being infiltrated. We couldn't get into the room yet to bug it, but we have a couple officers in custodial outfits going in to plant one shortly. If you want to be in on the bust be at room 1035 by eleven and don't look too suspicious."

"No problem, I'll just stagger down the hall like a drunk and come to the door. Are you going to let the men take the women, or stop them in the room?"

"We're going to play it by ear. I'd like to find out where they are going, so I may let them go. I hope Buck and Mac are away from the area when that happens."

"What if they drug the women?"

"They've been warned about drinking anything. One of the officers is going to actually drink; the others are going to pretend. If the one woman starts to feel like she is going out, the rest will pretend also. We have it all covered so far. I just don't like unknowns."

"Your people are all professional, they'll do the job. Besides, you have plenty of back-up, so you can pull the plug anytime if it looks bad."

"Yes, we have good people. I hope all goes well and we can find the boys and shut down this fucker. Dark will regret his coming to Vegas."

We finished and hung up. Lacey looked to me, I told her Mac was going to be all right.

"He better or I'm coming for you," she said with an evil grin.

*

Chapter 11

Jacob Dark had been to four different jewelry stores before he rested in his car staring at the last one he had entered. He pulled his cell phone and made a call.

"I've got a good one, get Kenny and Ben and meet me at our arranged spot. We can hit this one tonight." He hung up and put the phone away. He started the car and drove out of the parking lot of the large Jewelry store, heading to the restaurant where he would meet his men.

~~*~~

Earl was at our door by six and eager to go see what would happen at the Luxor with Buck and Mac.

"A bit early aren't you?" I asked.

"I just wanted to spend some quality time with my favorite people." Penny heard that from the couch and laughed out loud. "Hey, that offends me," Earl responded.

"You are offensive," I said, "Come on in and get comfortable, we're just watching TV waiting for eleven o'clock to get here."

"Eleven, is that when we roll?"

"You can roll, we'll drive. Lynn said to meet

them at the Luxor at eleven o'clock. Buck and Mac are bringing the police women by midnight."

"Why so late?"

"The carnival closes by then so they will be at the Luxor by midnight."

"Makes sense, whatcha watching?" he said glancing at the TV.

"Make yourself comfortable, we've been channel surfing, there's not a lot on."

Earl went to an easy chair and plopped down, "No beer," he said when he saw the Pepsi bottles on our snack tables.

"Nope, I'm driving tonight and want to keep a clear head in case this goes sour. Do you want one?"

"I'll take a Pepsi too." I knew he wanted a beer but he was being wise to wait.

We sat watching a cop show as Earl complained about the plot. I just told him to shut up.

~~*~~

Dark Carnival Murders

Buck and Mac were closing down the round-up and saw the women coming up the midway. Buck called to Mac and he came over.

"Ladies, how are you doing tonight?" Buck asked as the four women approached. They were dressed to party in tight, flashy clothes. Buck thought they were looking a little too much like hookers, but since they worked in vice, it was probably standard dress for them.

The lead officer answered, "We are ready to party." She looked around and saw there was no one close enough to hear, "I'm Kim, this is Tina, Mary and Lindsey. I'm wired so stay close to me to pick up conversations. Lindsey is going to be our designated drinker, we'll just pretend. Watch her for any sign of drugs in her drinks. Are we ready to go?"

Buck gave his famous walrus grin and they went to their vehicles. Mac was driving his pickup and the women would follow in their car. They drove out from the carnival grounds and up Vegas Boulevard. The Luxor was just up from the south end of the strip, so the ride didn't take long. They parked and Buck pulled the paper from his pocket that Skeeter gave him earlier in the day, it had the room number. They entered the huge pyramid shaped building and found the elevators to the tenth floor.

~~*~~

In one of the side rooms, Lynn was listening to their conversations as they came in range of the receiver. She nodded to me and Earl as we stood by listening. We had arrived about a half hour prior to Buck's entrance, waiting for them. Penny decided to stay home; she was tired and not wanting to get in the middle of a gun fight if things went wrong.

~~*~~

Buck and his party came to the door of their room and Buck knocked. The door was opened by one of the carnies that Buck recognized, but didn't know his name. The man smiled and said to come in. Buck let the women go in first, then Mac. The man identified himself as Louie, said to the women to make themselves comfortable and then pulled Buck and Mac aside.

"The plan has been changed, we're not grabbing anyone tonight."

Buck was startled when he heard that. "Why weren't we told about this at the carnival, would have saved a lot of time."

"Things came up at the last minute, no time to get word to you."

"What about these women?"

"Hey, you got a luxury room and four hot women, use your imagination." the greasy man grinned, showing a mouthful of teeth that needed pulling.

Buck was now desperate, "Well, we could take the women to the place where they need to go."

"Nah, everyone is going to be busy at the jewelry store. So there won't be anyone to take care of the women."

"Jewelry store, what's up?"

"Oh yeah, you're new, Dark likes to hit a couple jewelry stores in the towns we're in, helps build our retirement funds," he laughed and walked out the door.

"Well, fuck," Buck exploded after Louie was gone.

Kim came over and asked, "What's up?"

"The snatch has been cancelled, Dark is committing other crimes and he can't be bothered with us."

"There's going to be no kidnapping tonight?"

"That's what I'm told."

Buck heard a banging on the room door, he figured it was Lynn and opened the door. He was right.

Lynn entered and said, "I sent a couple men to follow Louie, maybe we'll catch Dark pulling his crime." She wasn't happy.

"You heard that through the wire while Kim was across the room?" Buck asked.

"We have good equipment. Now we need to regroup and find out what Dark is up to. This sucks and was a total waste of resources. Weber is going to have a nut when he sees the overtime on this."

"Well if we can find out what jewelry store Dark is hitting, it may be a save."

"I told Warren to call when he got a fix on the store, we'll head out as soon as he has something."

Lynn turned to the female officers and said, "I'd like to thank you for coming out, but stay prepared in case we have to go again."

The women left silently and Kim went to the other room to have her wire removed. We just stood in the room waiting for Warren to call.

"Wow, nice view from up here," Earl said as he looked out the window overlooking the strip all the way up to the Stratosphere.

"If we could open the window you could slide down the side of the pyramid," I joked.

"I've been on a real pyramid in Egypt, on a mission to stop a terrorist. We got our man and I got to see the top of the pyramid."

"If you want to go to the top of this one, I won't stop you," I said with a laugh.

Lynn said, "You two should start your own comedy routine, I know the entertainment director for the Golden Nugget."

"Hey, where's Deacon? I forgot all about him." I asked.

"He's on a mission, to close down an escort service operating illegally out of Circus, Circus," Lynn said.

"Hooker clowns?" I laughed.

"Shut up Jim, Deacon is…" Before she finished, her cell phone buzzed. She grabbed her phone, looked at the caller ID and smiled, then answered.

"Warren, talk to me." She listened for a moment and hung up. She yelled to her men, now in the hallway, to head out. Buck and Mac said they were staying in the room for the night, it was better than the camper, so Earl and I followed the cops. She gave the address to everyone in the elevator on the way down.

We went to our cars and drove up the boulevard to Flamingo Road and east to where Warren said the jewelry store was located. We pulled into the small strip mall and up to the store on the corner. It looked empty from the front, and there was no alarm sounding. Warren was parked down the lot and came up.

"Williams went around back, I haven't heard from him yet."

Lynn tried the door, it was locked. She told a couple of her men to watch the front and took the rest of us to the back. We carefully came around the side and saw a couple cars parked in the back alley. Lynn motioned to two of the uniforms to go around the back of a wall along the alley and to come up from the other side. They left and Lynn turned to Warren and asked, "Where's Williams?"

"He said he was going back here, God I hope they didn't grab him."

"That would be Williams, always a fuckup. Okay, let's go down to the door to see what's up?"

Lynn, Warren and two uniforms crept down the alley and up to the back door. Earl and I were behind them, with our weapons drawn. We got to the door of the jewelry store and Lynn told us to wait. She tried the door, it was also locked. She backed up and said to wait for anyone to come out.

We stood in the alley as Lynn called back to the precinct to get the listing for the owner of the jewelry store and to have them come down. I

102

looked around and only saw two cars, if Dark had a big hit going on here there should be more cars parked around. I looked down the alley and could see the two uniforms, waiting.

Suddenly the back door opened and we all brought up our weapons, a figure came out, it was Detective Williams.

*

Chapter 12

"Bernie! What's going on, who's inside?" Lynn demanded.

"No one," he said.

"Okay talk to me, what happened?"

"We followed Louie, he drove around the back and we stopped in the front. I told Greg that I was going around the back and when I got there I found the door wide open and Louie's car was gone. I carefully listened but heard nothing so went in and found the place empty. It's a mess in there; they must have left just before we arrived. "

Dark Carnival Murders

Lynn went past Williams and entered the building followed by everyone. The back room was torn up, boxes spilled and cabinets opened. It looked like they were in a rush to get whatever they needed.

I was studying the door, it didn't look like it was forced. It was a heavy steel door with two locks that had to be opened from the inside. I was sure the owner didn't forget to lock it. Lynn was now out front in the showroom and I went out there. The glass of all the display cases was smashed and it looked like they knew what to take, leaving the cheaper looking jewelry.

"This sucks worse than the cancelled kidnapping, we were too late. Damn, this is not good." She pulled her phone and called CSI to come in. We heard a noise at the front door and everyone jumped pulling their guns. A pasty faced man, short, fat and in poor shape entered. He looked shocked at the sight of all the guns pointed at him.

"Relax everyone!" Lynn yelled. She went to the man and asked if he was the owner, he said he was and his name was Joseph Lusk.

"What the hell happened here!" he yelled when he saw the mess. He went to the display cases and quickly examined the contents. "The fuckers got the good stuff. When did this happen?"

"We figure about an hour ago, we had a tip that this was going to go down, but we got here just after they left," Lynn said hoping to calm the man. He continued to rant and swear at the top of his lungs for about ten minutes searching the cases.

"Williams, will you take down Mr. Lusk's accounting of what was stolen, please?" Lynn asked the detective to get Lusk's attention away from the mess and to shut up his ranting.

Lynn left the showroom and went back to the rear door. She was checking it out when I came up, "It doesn't looked forced, maybe Dark had someone on the inside, who either opened it for them or left it unlocked?"

"I'm sure the employees would have noticed an extra person in the building. Unless one of the employees was in on it." She turned to Warren and asked, "Check with Lusk as to who was working today and how we can reach them." He went off as Lynn stepped into the alley. She knelt and looked around the ground. "Too many tire marks back here and none are distinct enough."

"Trying to take my job now, Lynn," came a voice from the doorway. It was Larry Wayne, the supervisor of CSI. "I'm glad you cleared the crime scene and kept all your people from walking around on it."

Lynn stood, embarrassed, "Sorry, we got here and it's been a bit hectic."

"It's all right, we'll work around your people," he said with a big smile.

Lynn went to the door just as Warren was coming up, "Get everyone out of there until CSI checks the building."

"Sure, Lusk said it was just him and his wife working today, no one else was in the building that he saw." He turned, went back in and chased everyone out.

"That he saw," I repeated. "Could Dark have gotten someone in the place to hide until after the store closed?"

"It's possible. We'll have to see if Lusk had security cameras running when he was closing up. Hopefully he did."

"I'm sure he did, he seems to be the nervous type about his store," Earl offered.

Lynn turned to Earl who was standing behind us by the door, "Are you still with us?"

"Yes I am. I once saw this in an old movie, circus comes to town and they distract the owner of a store while the bad guys slip a little person past the owner and he hides in a cabinet in the back room. He disables the alarm and opens the back door. Simple." Earl grinned like he solved the case.

"Little person? Like a midget?" Lynn asked.

"Can't call them midgets anymore, it offends them," I said.

"Geez, political correctness is running rampant. Does Dark have a little person in his troop of carnies?"

"It's possible," I said pulling my cell phone. "I'll call Buck to see."

I went off to the side of the alley as Buck answered. "Jimmy, this hotel room is nice. Mac is relaxing in the whirlpool."

"I hope he's not naked. Tell me, is there a little person who works for Dark?"

"Little person, you mean a midget? Yeah, Ben is a little person, stands about three-one, why?"

"Long story, I'll tell you later. Thanks and don't run up too big of a room bill, Dark might get upset."

I hung up and went back to Lynn, "Buck says they do have a little person in the carnival. But it's a stretch that he was involved."

"Hey, it's my theory. Let me have the glory of having figured it out," Earl said.

Lynn frowned, "Whatever, we need to do something. If I haul Dark and his people in for questioning because we knew he was going to pull this, that blows Buck and Mac's cover and we may never find the boys. We'll have to sit on this and make the kidnapping a priority. Buck needs to push Dark into going again with the women. Jim, call him back and see what he can do."

"Will do, give me a little time to set it up with him." I went back to the side and called Buck explaining everything that happened here and that he needed to prod Dark into going again on the kidnapping. He agreed and I hung up.

"He's going to do his best to get it going again," I said to Lynn.

"So it's a waiting game again, I'm so going to change occupations," Lynn moaned.

"Have you ever thought of becoming a stripper?" Earl said.

"Just who invited you to this party anyways?"

"Blame Jim, he brought me."

Lynn gave me a snarl and went back into the building. I smacked Earl on the shoulder and called him a putz. We followed her in and found that CSI was just finishing up. Lynn was talking to Larry Wayne and they had nothing much to go on. Larry said they found a few fingerprints on the alarm system but most were just smudges and the video tapes from the cameras were taken.

"Great, we have no video to watch now. They took care of everything. Warren, get on the computer and see if you can find any similar robberies in cities that Dark went through."

"Williams pulled a list of the route taken by the carnival, through registered permits, I can go with that," he said and started to go.

"Get on it and quickly." She went back to Larry and asked, "What's your expert opinion?"

"It's a mystery, had to be someone on the inside, no marks of forced entry. I'm sure Lusk didn't forget to turn on the alarm and lock the doors. You've got a mystery."

"We know who did it, but we can't touch them yet, they are connected to a more serious case of child abduction. We have to play this carefully," Lynn replied.

"Well, good luck, I'll call if we can come up with something." He went off after calling his people to the cars.

Lynn turned to me, "All we can do now is wait for Buck to pull a rabbit out of his hat. I'll have robbery alerted to other jewelry stores in the area, in case Dark tries it again."

My cell phone buzzed and I excused myself, it was Penny. "Hey babe, what's up? Why aren't you in bed, it's after one in the morning."

"I didn't know when you were coming back, Angelo stopped by earlier to say his Mom and Gino are in town, they arrived tonight. Angelo put them up in the Tropicana Hotel and Francis told him to tell me we are having a spa day tomorrow after I tape my show. I'm going to pick her up in the morning to take her to my studio to watch, then off to beauty land."

"I hope they can help you. I'm about finished here, I'll be home as soon as I can."

"Help me? Is there something wrong with me, huh? Do you think I need help? You better duck when you get home buddy." She hung up and I regretted trying to joke with her, but I knew she loved it.

I went back to Earl and said, "I'm done here, I'll take you back to your car and then I'll go fight with my lovely wife."

"What dumb thing did you say now?" he said with a laugh.

"Gino and Francis are in town, and Penny is going with Francis tomorrow for spa treatments."

"And you made a comment about her needing treatments."

"Close enough. Do you know any flower shops open this late?"

Earl looked back to the jewelry store and said, "No, but I know where you can get a nice

111

necklace for her." He busted out laughing and we went to my van.

*

Chapter 13

Finally arriving at my home, Earl drove off without making any more smart-ass comments. I went into the house and straight to the bedroom and found Penny sound asleep, so I didn't wake her. I felt bad that I hadn't called the Walkers earlier to let them know we were still on the case.

I took a quick shower in my bathroom and toweled off. Willy was standing in the doorway watching me and looking half asleep. I picked him up and put him on his Bates Motel chair and then I crawled into bed. I was asleep quickly.

Morning came and I could hear a commotion coming from the kitchen area and could smell something good. I threw on a robe and went out to find Penny and Angelo packing a picnic basket of food.

"I thought you were going to the studio, then to a spa? What's with the picnic basket?" I asked.

"Angelo is whipping up some snacks for us while we are at the studio. It's sort of a welcome to Vegas for Francis," Penny replied.

I looked in the basket and they had a bunch of tasty looking homemade pastries and assorted goodies.

"Angelo, you never cease to amaze me, you are a pastry chef too?" I asked.

"All good Italian chefs know how to make great cannoli's and other pastries. It's part of the tradition."

I started to reach in for one and Penny smacked my hand. I recoiled and went to the bread box to get my slices for toast.

"Angelo, what's Gino doing today?" I asked.

"Gee Mr. R., you don't really want to know. It's better that way."

"Gotcha, enough said." Ah, the life of a mob capo. Probably going to be mixing up cement for someone's shoes. "What are you going to be doing today?"

"I'm going to keep my mom company at the studio until they go to the spa, then I'll go visit a couple friends."

"Hey, did you find out anything from your gypsy friends about Dark and Cole?"

"Oh, yeah. Sorry I forgot, my contacts don't know either of them but they are still going to check for me. I'll let you know as soon as something pops."

"Thanks Angelo." I turned to Penny and said, "I'll be with Lynn and Deacon today, call if you need me."

"I'll be relaxing and being pampered by soothing hands today, so don't bother me. Angelo is going to drive us in the mini-limo." She kissed me and then said to Angelo, "Shall we go?" They went out to the car, which Angelo brought out earlier. I looked to Willy and said, "Guess it's just us two, big guy."

I drove by the office building to drop off Willy for Lacey to watch and check my messages, there were none. I didn't know if that was good or bad, but it was no fun being ignored.

"Jim, is Mac going to be finished anytime soon?" Lacey asked as I came out to the lobby.

"Why, are you getting horny without him around?"

"Hey, that's personal. I'm just wanting to know so I can plan our lives. I want to make sure that Jessie doesn't go off to college before Mac gets home."

"Jessie's not old enough for college and Mac will be home in plenty of time. You'll be the first to know when he's finished." I left the lobby and went back to my office to called the Walkers. I knew nothing I could say would help them, but just my voice on the phone so that they knew I hadn't given up may give them a little comfort. They held up well.

After I finished giving the Walkers a bit of hope, my cell phone rang, it was Lynn. "Good Morning," I said as I answered.

"It would be a better morning if we had Dark in custody. I hate letting him skate for the jewelry robbery but I accept the reason for letting it go for now. It's been two days since the boys have gone missing, this is not good. Get on Buck to start the ball rolling again, we need to find out where they take the women and hope the boys are there."

"I'll call him shortly. Have you contacted robbery division about possible hits on other jewelry stores?"

"I have and they understand the situation. They will do what they can to prevent the robberies, but not apprehend Dark and his crew. Just enough to scare them off, and not arrest anyone for now. Hopefully today we can get the women back into the hotel. Warren checked and said that the Luxor room is being reserved for another day, so that may be good."

"I'll put a bug in Buck's ear to get it going. I'll call when I have something for you." We finished and I hung up, and then dialed Buck. It was still early enough for him to be in the camper. He came on after two rings. "Hey Buck, can you talk?"

"Sure can Jimmy, what's the word?" he said with a pleasant response.

"Dark got away with the robbery last night, Lynn is holding off pulling him in for questioning, she doesn't want to give your cover away. You need to prod Dark into going again with the women, we need to get to the boys, time is running out. The longer we take the worse it could be. Dark isn't going to murder them, they are more valuable to him alive. We just need to stop this before they

116

are taken somewhere and we'll never find them."

"I'll get on Dark first thing this morning. I was just waiting to hear from you."

"Good, so go to it and let me know what's going on."

"Will do," he said and hung up. It was now up to him.

~~*~~

Buck and Mac went flying out of the camper, headed right to Dark's trailer and the old woman behind the cage waved them through to Dark's office. He was sitting at his desk with Skeeter standing by as they were checking the jewelry they snatched.

"Ah Buck, my sincere apologies to you for the abrupt cancellation of our little kidnapping last night. Things came up quickly, and we had to take the priority of obtaining quick funds. I've arranged for the nabbing to go again tonight. Did you and the ladies have a good time last night?" Dark spoke with his evil grin never wavering.

117

"No, they were a bit put off that the party was canceled, they left shortly after."

"Well, we'll do better tonight, I have a client who is in need of women for his palace in Dubai. Pick some really stacked females, he likes busty women."

"We'll do our best. I have a question."

"Ask away my friend."

"The cops were asking around yesterday, about some missing kids, are we into grabbing children too?"

"Why, do you object, do you have some morals about it?" Dark's grin faded a little.

"Hell no, I just like to know what's going down before I make a fool of myself to the cops."

Dark smiled a little more now, "Yes, good point, we do provide younger ones at a good price. We have three now that we will be auctioning off shortly. If you'd like to watch how we do this, you are more than welcome to join us."

"An auction, I like that. Ever been to a slave auction Mac?" Buck said to his partner.

"Nope, just seen some in the movies, sounds interesting. Like cattle to the slaughter," Mac replied holding back his hate for Dark.

"Count us in, when is this taking place?" Buck said turning back to Dark.

"Tomorrow night after we close down, I have a number of clients coming in, I may need your help to keep them happy."

"You got it. Well, we have work to do," Buck said, and he motioned to Mac to leave. He stopped and turned back, "Let me know about the party tonight, that all is going to go as planned."

"You got it Buck," Dark replied and the big men left the trailer.

Dark turned to Skeeter, "It was a little strange that the cops arrived so quickly after our break-in last night, like they knew. I think we need to watch our two new friends a little closer."

*

Chapter 14

My cell phone buzzed and I checked the ID, it was Buck. "Speak to me," I said as I answered.

"I'll talk quick, I'm in my phone booth."

"Port-a-potty?"

"You got it. The nabbing is back on for tonight, send the women out or four different ones. I don't think Louie paid much attention to the last group, but may as well be safe. Now the bonus! The boys are still alive and in the city. Dark is going to auction them off in a special showing tomorrow night. Mac and I have been invited but I don't know where yet."

I took a big sigh hearing that they were all right. "Okay buddy, do what you have to do and I'll get Lynn set up again. Same deal I presume?"

"As far as I know, Dark wasn't very talkative. I'll call again when I get more, later," he said and hung up.

I put my cell phone back in my pocket and

grabbed the desk phone to call Lynn. She came on quickly.

"Good news, the boys are still alive and nearby, but Buck doesn't know where. The nabbing is set to go again tonight, so have your girls ready."

I could hear Lynn let out a little whoop and then she said, "Best news I've had in the last two days. Know anything more about them?"

"Buck said they are going to be auctioned off tomorrow night, I presume to lecherous, creepy men who need little boys but don't want to grab the kids themselves."

"Bastards, I'm going to love busting that sale. Call me as soon as you find out something. Now shall I send out the same women?"

"Buck suggested four new ones, he doesn't think the weasel who was there really got a good look at the women but to be on the safe side."

"Got it, I'll get back to you if we have anything on this side." She hung up and I sat back thinking about calling the Walkers and the Feltons, but I decided to wait. Nothing worse for the parents to get hope, then have this all blow up. I'll call as soon as all three boys are in our custody.

I stood from my desk and went out to the lobby, Lacey was busy typing and caught me out of the corner of her eye. She jumped but didn't scream.

"What," I said. "I'm not announcing my arrival in the lobby every time I come out."

"You noticed I didn't scream, so I'm getting used to you now. So what do you want?"

"I'm going to take a ride and get something to eat. Just so you know we may have this sewn up by tomorrow night."

"About time, I was getting Jessie ready to go off to Harvard," she said with a smile.

"Harvard, how much do I pay you?"

"Well with the raise you gave me, not enough."

"I doubled your salary, and you still aren't making enough?"

"Chill Jim, I'm kidding. I'm happy with the raise and I'm going to send Jessie to UNLV so she is still close by."

"She has a good number of years before she can even go there."

"She's smart like me, so she'll get in early."

"She's not your blood relation."

"So, she picks up from me every day, she's a fast learner."

"Whatever, I'm out of here."

I went out the door to my van and drove over to Sonic for a burger and onion rings. I enjoyed my meal and then headed to visit Lynn and Deacon. I went into the back door of the precinct and the officer at the sign-in counter waved me through. It was nice to feel like I was part of the team. I had helped with enough cases to qualify as being part of the LVMPD. I still had my auxiliary police badge, which no one asked for it's return, so I considered myself to be part of the force.

I didn't find Lynn or Deacon in her office, but Deacon was now part of Vice so he didn't hang out here much, I would miss him. I could go over to Vice and visit, maybe check out the women they pulled in, but Penny would smell it on me, so not a good idea.

Warren was at his desk and saw me. "Lynn is

in with Weber, I hope she gets out alive."

I went over and sat next to Warren's desk and asked, "Now why would Weber harm Lynn?"

"He's bothered by the fact that Lynn is homicide and the case she's following is kidnapping and human trafficking, plus now robbery. I'm sure she'll wiggle her way out of it, Weber is getting soft lately. Maybe he's losing it, he's been on the force forever."

"He's a strange little man, but he's harmless," I said. I looked over to the lobby hallway and saw Lynn coming out to the squad room. She saw me and waved me to her office, I went.

"So what did Weber have to say?" I asked.

"He fumed about the cost of our busted bust last night but I explained the whole case to him and he's going along with me. He worries about missing children too. He's assigning a small task force to this, but with what you told me, we may be able to clear this up soon."

"I hope we aren't disappointed. We'll see how the kidnapping goes tonight, hopefully it won't queer the deal for tomorrow night. We need to think this out carefully," I said.

"You're right, if we grab the kidnappers tonight they may move the boys somewhere else. I may need to have the women be kidnapped for the duration just to keep this thing going. I hope they can take it."

"You're people are pros, they can do it. Besides if they take the women to the same place as the kids, our problems are solved."

"I hope so, I want to bring this case to an end, and we need to get the boys back safely."

I looked over to see Deacon walking down the hallway towards us. He grinned when he saw me sitting by Lynn's desk in his usual chair.

"Taking my place now," he said as he came in the room.

"No one can replace you pal. Are you sick of the hookers yet?" I said.

"Close," he said with a side glance to Lynn. "The women are not anything I'd want to spend time with. They aren't the finest females in the world. Not like my wife," he threw in for luck.

"You are one smart man, bunny bear," Lynn said with a grin.

"Please don't start the bunny bear stuff again. I'm still trying to live down the last time you were mad at me and let everyone in the squad hear you call me that. I'm even getting it over in vice now."

"Sorry my dear, I can't call it back now so just wear it as a badge of honor."

"Bunny bear is not a badge of honor. So how's the case going? Find the boys yet?" he said changing the subject.

"Close, but still no cigar. Buck told me today that the boys are being auctioned off tomorrow night," I said. "At least we know the boys are still alive and close."

"Are you still in need of the women for the kidnapping?"

"Yep, it's going on again tonight, but we have to be careful in grabbing the criminals so they don't change the auction tomorrow and we lose the boys," Lynn said with a sigh.

My cell phone buzzed, I pulled it from my pocket and saw by the caller ID it was Angelo. I excused myself and went out to the squad room to answer.

"Talk to me my friend," I said.

126

"Just wanted to fill you in on the situation with Mom and Penny, they are done with the show and I dropped them off at WonderSpa, they're probably soaking in mud by now."

"Thanks for the update but you don't have to keep me informed."

"That's not the only reason I called, I got word from my gypsy friends, they say they can't find anything on the man called Jacob Dark, but they tracked down Lucius Cole."

"Where's he at?"

"In Vegas, the gypsies say there is no real Jacob Dark, it's a front for the carnival. Jacob Dark is actually Lucius Cole."

*

Chapter 15

"Oh man, that is great info, thanks, I'll tell Lynn. Anything else you have?"

"Nope, that's all I got," he said.

"Good, have a nice visit with your friends, or you can stop by and follow us."

"Sure, if I get bored listening to shop talk by my leg breaker friends," he said with a loud laugh, then hung up.

I went back to Lynn's office and sat on the chair I vacated. "Got some good news," I said.

"Okay, talk."

"There is no one named Jacob Dark." I sat waiting for a moment.

"Jim cut the suspense, what are you talking about?"

"Jacob Dark is Lucius Cole. Dark is the carnival's name and he's calling himself by that name."

"Okay that's interesting; I guess he wants to keep up a front. That must be why Warren couldn't get anything on him as a person. I never trusted criminals who use an alias."

"This doesn't change much other than we know he is hiding behind the name. We just know more about the man now. Okay, I don't feel like sitting here until the sting tonight so I'm going to go back to the office and try to look like I work there." I stood and saluted, then left.

"Same room, same time," Lynn yelled to me, I responded by waving my hand.

I drove out Industrial road to our new office, parked and went in. The cowbell that Lacey attached to the back door clanged, letting Lacey know someone came in. She was probably watching the security monitor to see who it was. I waved to the camera as I went to my office and sat at my new desk. She came bouncing down the hallway and into my room.

"I got to talk to Mac this morning; he was telling me they may be done tomorrow night. This is good, I was starting to forget what he looked like."

"Lacey, you are such a drama queen. Maybe you can get your own show at Caesar's Palace, after Rod Stewart, or is Celine Dion back yet?"

"She's coming back, but I don't think she'd want me after her show, people may forget about her," she laughed and went off.

"I'm surrounded by loonies," I said and checked my email on my computer.

~~*~~

Buck was just slowing down the ride when two women came up and said the phrase he was waiting for. He smiled and gave them the instructions for tonight. They went off as Buck and Mac went back to running the round-up.

From across the midway, Skeeter was watching Buck closely. He had seen the meeting of the women and thought it was a bit brief for trying to coax the females to a party. Maybe Dark was right, they may have some other motive for their actions.

Skeeter went off to report to Dark.

~~*~~

My phone buzzed, it was Penny. "Hey sexy, are you all primped and poised now?"

"My body tingles with energy. You better be ready tonight for a little action."

"Well, I may be a little late tonight, the kidnapping is going on again so just have a good time with Francis and I'll be home when I can."

"You are just a kill-joy aren't you?"

"I'll make it up to you."

"You better or I'll have Gino have a serious talk with you." She laughed as I asked her where she was. She said at the house for now, they were going to a show at the Flamingo. Angelo was still driving.

I said to have a good time and we'd talk later, then hung up. I felt a little guilty having our mob friends in town and I was busy. I'm sure Angelo is probably filling them in on what was going on.

Earl walked into my office and sat. "What's up?"

131

"Well, the snatch is going on again tonight, if it doesn't get canceled at the last minute." I explained everything new that came up today.

"So, same situation as before?"

"Yep, if nothing screws up. Are you still in for it?"

"You bet, I'm ready to take down a few kidnappers."

"But that's the thing, we can't take them down without giving away our intentions and screwing up the auction of the boys. We have to walk through this carefully."

"Got it, let me know when we are heading over to the Luxor, I'll be ready."

"You haven't said much about Paula? Is she still with you?"

"Hell yeah, she's really happy to be here in Vegas. She has this secret desire to be a dancer on stage, I need to talk to Buck to see if Maria can get her a try-out for her show."

"It's a topless show, do you think you can share Paula's great breasts with the rest of the world?"

"What do you know about Paula's breasts?" Earl gave me a big grin.

"I may be married to Penny but I'm not dead, well, close to it."

"I'll tell her you said that."

"Go ahead, she's used to me by now. So shall we go get something to eat and kill time till we go save the world?"

"Sounds good to me. I suppose we're going to Sonic?"

"Let's go to Carl's Jr. this time, just for a change."

We went out after I told Lacey that we would be gone the rest of the day. We headed to the closest Carl's Jr. and ate, then I drove by the house to see if the women were still there, they were.

"Sweetie, you just couldn't stay away, and you brought my boy toy," she said with a laugh and kissed me, then Earl.

"Hey stop that, he doesn't deserve a kiss. Hello Francis, how are you doing?" I said to her as she came over to give me a hug. Angelo was standing in the kitchen and came out to the living room to greet us.

"I'm doing very well Jim. I hear you are chasing down some despicable person who kidnaps children?" Francis said.

"Yes we are. We have an ongoing investigation tonight to stop human trafficking. Sounds like when we were out in New York," I said.

She laughed and said, "Yes, and you got shot as I remember, don't do that again."

"I have Earl to jump between me and a bullet tonight."

He looked at me, "I'm sorry, but when did I sign up for that?"

"You know you love me," I said and turned back to Francis, "Where's Gino?"

"He's doing his business. I don't get involved, I learned early in the life that the men take care of the business and we enjoy the spoils. Are you hoping to get the boys back?"

134

"Always, I'm sure we will. Thanks for your concern, now we have to go back out to fight the bad guys," I said before I thought that Gino was technically a bad guy according to the law. "We need to do something fun before you go home," I said changing the subject. "I'll let Penny plan something special. Our case should be tied up by tomorrow night, we have good info that we can find the boys."

"Wonderful Jim, please bring them home safely," Francis said.

~~*~~

Closing time at the carnival. Buck and Mac had shut down the ride and saw the women coming up the midway. They greeted them and then went off to their cars. Skeeter was watching at a distance, then followed them.

Buck pulled into the Luxor parking structure and parked. He guided the women, new ones this time from the last, to the lobby and up to the tenth floor again. They arrived at the door after passing our door. Lynn had the door open slightly and

Buck saw her, just to let him know we were ready. Earl and I were standing by the table where they had the communication equipment set up. We could hear Buck talking to Mary, the female cop with the wire.

"You're going to enjoy this party girl," he was saying as he knocked at the door. Lynn had the room bugged last night, it still was working and we could hear the men in the room giving orders to be ready.

Everyone in our room was tense, we had no idea what to expect, but we were ready. Lynn gave Mary a code word in case things went bad. She listened closely for it.

The door opened and Louie was there to greet them. "Hey Buck come on in and bring your friends."

Everyone entered the room, there were three men standing nearby, Mary asked if this was the whole party?

Louie looked to her and said, "Be patient, we haven't even begun. Now please sit and relax."

The women went to the big couch and sat. They were all lookers and Louie said to Buck, "Good choice, my friend, now get lost."

Buck was taken by surprise and said, "Don't you need us to help?"

"Nope, get out of here, we'll take it from here."

Buck didn't want to queer the deal so he looked to Mac and said to follow him. Louie opened the door as they went out. He closed the door as Mary asked where they were going. The snooping equipment gave us their voices.

"They are just going out to get some refreshments." He turned to the bedroom door as it opened, Skeeter walked out.

The women gave Skeeter a surprised look as he pointed a gun and said, "Ladies, I need you to put your hands up and close your mouths."

*

Chapter 16

I carefully opened the suite door to look out and see where Buck and Mac went to. They were still standing in the hallway talking. Buck saw me, looked back to the door they just came out of and moved over towards me. I opened the door for them and they entered.

"What's going on in the room?" Buck asked.

Lynn smiled and said, "The game is afoot," quoting Sherlock Holmes.

"Who's foot? What do feet have to do with the case?" Buck was confused.

"Buck, someone has the women held with a threat. I'm imagining he has a gun on them. The kidnapping begins," I said.

Buck went to the communication equipment and listened. We could hear Skeeter giving orders to the other men.

"That's Skeeter's voice, I didn't see him in the room when we took the ladies in," Buck said.

"It sounded like he was in another room and after you left he came out."

Skeeter's voice from the other room said, "Okay ladies, put all your cell phones on the table along with your purses."

"I hope he doesn't frisk them," Earl spoke up.

"Mary has the wire and the safe word so be ready if she says it," Lynn said.

"What is the safe word?" Buck asked.

"Biscuits," Lynn replied.

"Biscuits? That's the word, who thinks these things up?" Buck laughed.

"Quiet, Skeeter's giving more commands."

From the speaker we could hear him saying, "Okay ladies, here's what is going down. If you cooperate you'll live long and productive lives. Otherwise you die. Now we are all going out of this room, each of these men will escort you and I'll take this lovely lady." It sounded like he yanked one of the women up from the couch and then continued. "Now if any of you decide to run, or open your mouths to get help, I'll shoot this bitch in the head. You don't want to be responsible for her death, now do you?"

We could hear the women agreeing.

"Do you have a tracker on Mary?" Earl asked.

"Yes we do, it's in her belt. It's hidden well, unless they have an electronic de-bugging device. I got electronics division in the precinct watching her. They'll report back when they can confirm a route from the hotel."

Skeeter was now speaking loudly, "Okay everyone, get up and pair with the men, we are going out now and I don't want any problems, or she dies, understand?"

We could hear agreements, then they were moving about in the room. We could hear the door open and Lynn got on her walkie-talkie and asked someone named Dave if he had them on the radar. He confirmed that they were on the move and would keep her posted. Lynn clipped the unit to her belt and put an earpiece in her ear.

We moved to the door, Lynn listened and then carefully opened it. She couldn't see them but heard them heading down the hall in the opposite direction from us. Lynn stuck her head out the door and saw them go into the stairwell door. She said to move, we went out the door.

Lynn pulled her cell phone and hit a speed dial number, "George, have you got eyes on them?"

I knew she had arranged with the hotel security to follow them on the cameras all over the hotel. The man on the other end of the call told Lynn they were in the stairwell and heading down.

"They would have to be going to the ground floor, let's take the elevator down to greet them," Lynn said as Warren, Williams, Earl and I, followed by Buck and Mac, went to the elevator and pushed the button for the first floor.

We stood waiting... annoyed that the thing didn't move faster. Lynn was still listening to the security report of the men, they were almost to the ground floor. We burst out from the elevator and around the corner to see the four men and four women come out of the stairwell door and head for the exit. Lynn thanked the man in the security room and we followed, but not too close.

Buck could see Skeeter and I said to him that maybe he should back off in case Skeeter looked back and saw him. He agreed, so he and Mac stopped and went off the side of the room behind a row of slot machines.

Dark Carnival Murders

Lynn was listening through the earpiece to Dave back in the precinct who was following the GPS and reporting their progress. She led us out to the parking lot and we waited until they had gotten in a very long limo. Warren and Williams went off quickly to get their cars so we could follow. We stood waiting for something to happen; the limo started up and pulled out of the parking, heading out to Las Vegas Boulevard.

Two unmarked cars pulled up with Warren and Williams driving, we piled in. Lynn asked Dave where they were headed and the man on the other end said they turned south on the Boulevard. Lynn gave the details to Warren and he drove out.

It was after midnight and dark so it was easier to tail the limo without being seen. Lynn said Dave reported that they were still going south; Warren kept going until we spotted the car and then he pulled back since we had them on GPS. Dave reported that the limo had suddenly turned left into McCarran Airport's commercial business area. Warren carefully turned into the drive across the median and drove through the gates, pulling around to the side of the commercial hangers where they ran the private flights out of Vegas. He parked as Dave reported that the bad guys had stopped.

Everyone piled out of the unmarked cars and

carefully went around the hangers where we could see the limo parked by a very expensive Airstream jet. We watched as the men pulled the women out of the limo and handed them over to three other men standing by the plane.

"They're taking them out of the area quickly. Crap, we don't want to lose them but we also don't want to give away our sting to Dark. We have to time this closely," Lynn was speaking, "Warren get on your phone and call the McCarran Airport security and have them tell the tower to delay that plane from leaving. Get the tail number and call."

Warren went off to make the call as we watched. "If Dark's men leave the airport before the plane takes off, we can get the women back and lock down these men for kidnapping, and Dark will never know what we did."

Warren came back and told us the tower was going to put the plane in a delayed hold. We waited until Skeeter and his men got back in the limo and drove off. "Williams, go watch and let me know when they are out of the airport," Lynn said and Williams went off.

"This may work," I said.

"So why do I feel like something is going to screw up," she said with a grimace.

143

Dark Carnival Murders

We got the word that Dark's men had driven off the property and we relaxed. Lynn led the charge towards the jet, but as we were almost there the thing started up and was moving now.

"Crap, they're supposed to wait for the tower to clear them," Lynn yelled over the roar of the jets. "Follow me," she said as she ran back to the cars. She got in the driver's seat and started it up. Warren got into the passenger seat as Earl and I jumped in the back. Williams went to the other car. Lynn sped out towards the now moving jet as it left the tarmac and headed out to the runway.

Lynn, followed by Williams, sped down the runway towards the accelerating jet. "The bastard is going to break airport regs and take off without authorization. So he thinks." She accelerated faster now and was pulling alongside of the jet. Warren had his window down and was showing his badge to the cockpit, it didn't do much, the jet kept going.

Lynn pushed the car hard and finally got ahead of the jet and turned sharply into the path of the beast. We all jumped from the car as the jet was hitting its brakes narrowly missing Lynn's car by inches. We all had our guns trained on the plane as Williams pulled up next to the jet. We waited for something to happen inside.

We could hear a number of gunshots and saw flashes from the window of the jet. My heart skipped a couple beats as we waited. After a few minutes, the gangplank lowered and we aimed our weapons towards the opening. Suddenly Mary came out followed by her women and Lynn went running to them.

"What happened?" she yelled as the jet was shutting down its engines.

"Assholes, they were more interested in watching you guys out here, we got the drop on them from behind. Just four helpless women, no threat to the big bad guys," she laughed with a sigh of relief.

*

Chapter 17

Lynn had called for backup and the men on the plane were being dragged off. Lynn then placed a call to Bill Kestor, the FBI agent out in Florida, and explained why she woke him at an ungodly hour. He was appreciative and said he would get hold of his counterpart in Vegas and have them investigate the human trafficking angle.

Lynn came to Earl and I, "Well, I think we got this part of the situation taken care of. Kidnapping, robbery and child endangerment, Dark is really racking them up."

"How are you going to keep this under wraps so Dark doesn't hear back from the people he sold these women to?" I asked.

"I talked to Bill Kestor, FBI, and he agreed to see about delaying info about the jet. As far as the people in Dubai will be concerned, the jet was delayed for engine problems. We just have to delay for one more day. Tonight is the auction and if we can take that down and get the boys back, the FBI can move in on the slavers. The men on the plane will spend a quiet night in Homeland Security cells here at the airport." Lynn explained. "Next, we need to get Buck to find out where the auction is to take place."

As if on cue, Buck and Mac drove up in their camper, after calling me earlier to find out where we were. They parked and came over to us.

"One more night and hopefully this will end," Buck said.

"You have to get the info for the auction to us as soon as you hear from Dark," Lynn said.

"What if he doesn't tell me?" Buck asked.

Lynn thought for a moment, "We may need to hook you up for GPS. I'll have Dave set it up for you."

"Will that thing follow me to the john?" Buck laughed.

"I hope not, but we're lucky it has no sound capabilities. We don't need to hear you fart," I said.

"Gentlemen, it's now after one in the morning, I think we can call it a night," Lynn said as airport security was putting the men from the jet into a van to be taken to the office of the airport Homeland Security to be detained.

Dark Carnival Murders

We all agreed and went to our vehicles. I drove Earl back to the office where he left his car and he drove off. I headed home and the house was dark by the time I got there. I didn't hear the driveway alarm going off so I presumed Penny didn't set it. I parked the van and went in the front door to find Willy sitting in the middle of the kitchen looking half-asleep.

"Are you hungry, is that why you're in here?" I said standing at the door to the kitchen.

"He and I are both hungry, did you bring any food home with you?" Penny said coming up behind me. "Did you get your kidnappers?"

I put my arms around her and pulled her in tightly, "Yes, we did. They are on ice for now until we get the boys back tonight. I hope this ends on a good note. As to food, I didn't know I was supposed to bring any."

"It's alright; I don't expect you to think of mundane things like feeding your wife and son. I'll whip up something for us. I presume you haven't eaten?"

"Had a Carl's Jr. burger earlier but I could use a meal. Are you going to wake Angelo or attempt to cook yourself?"

She whacked my arm and went into the kitchen, I followed.

We had microwave treats, Penny's best way of cooking and then headed to bed. Willy was put on his Bate's Motel chair and circled a few times before plopping down with a snort. We were in bed quickly and Penny snuggled close. She was asleep before I could even get comfortable, she could do that very easily. I lay there thinking about what may go down tonight; hopefully it would come to an end. I slept well this morning.

Morning, Penny was already out of bed, I didn't hear anything from the kitchen so I figured Angelo was busy with his mother and Gino. Then I figured Penny would be back to her bowl of oatmeal and I would be toasting slices of bread. We shouldn't get used to Angelo's cooking, he may move any day now. I thought about fronting the money so Angelo could open his restaurant, but I'd hate to lose him as a bodyguard. I'd ask him about it to see how he felt.

I got up and went to my bathroom and readied my body for the day. I was shaved, showered, groomed and dressed to go out and fight crime. Penny was now banging pans and I went out to see what she was up to. Surprisingly, she cooked up pancakes for us.

"Well, I see Angelo has rubbed off on you."

She smiled and put the dish in front of me. We ate and it wasn't half bad, then I collected the plates and we kissed at the door to go to our jobs.

"Are you going to see Francis today?" I asked as we walked to our vehicles.

"Later, she's spending time with Angelo this morning, they are sightseeing."

"Good, I'll see you later."

I came through the back door of the office setting off the cowbell and waved to the camera. I went to my office and sat checking my email, nothing again. I was offended that no one even cared enough to send me spam.

Lacey came to the door and said, "Talked to Mac this morning, it's good you guys are going to get the boys back."

"I'm just hoping all goes well. Any messages for me?"

"Nope, nobody cares enough to leave you messages."

"Thanks for the ray of sunshine, go do some work to earn your raise."

She laughed and went off.

I picked up the phone to call the Walkers and the Feltons, being cautious about what I was going to tell them. They both responded well and I gave them some hope. I sat back as my cell phone buzzed, caller ID said it was Lynn.

"I hope you don't have any bad news," I said.

"Well, not for the boys, but there was another jewelry store hit last night. Same M.O., door unlocked, no alarm."

"Dark is spreading his men out. I thought robbery was going to watch the stores?"

"We couldn't watch all of them, Vegas just has too many, they happened to hit one we didn't have eyes on. I don't know if they knew we were watching or just lucky. Heard from Buck yet?"

"No, I'm just waiting, hopefully they'll find out something."

Earl walked in and I signaled him to sit. "Where are you?" I asked Lynn.

"I'm at the jewelry store trying to get any connection to Dark. Robbery is cooperating in this since we have a common connection. Why don't you stop by and do some snooping. It's near the corner of Tropicana and Decatur, watch for all the black and whites. "

"We'll do that."

We?" she said cautiously.

"Yeah, Earl just came in."

"Oh goody, we really need him this morning," she laughed and hung up, I put my phone back in my pocket.

"What?" Earl asked. "You were talking about me."

"It's nothing really, she's happy you are on the case."

"That's not what she really said is it?"

"Earl she likes you, even if you annoy her."

"I do no such thing, do I?," Earl said with indignation.

"Yesterday you suggested she become a
152

stripper, she's a sensitive person right now since she's pregnant."

"Oh yeah, I forgot about that. I'll try to be more understanding."

"Shall we go check out another robbery of a jewelry store?"

"Again? Boy, Dark must need the money."

I went out to the lobby and told Lacey we were leaving and she said, "About time."

I just ignored her and led Earl out to the van. We arrived at the store and found Lynn standing with a couple suits. I presumed they were official.

We came up and Lynn introduced them, they were from robbery division. "Jim we have another problem, the store owner says one of his employees was in the store all night doing inventory, now she's missing."

"Think she was taken by Dark's men or was she in on it?"

"Don't really know at this point, but she's a lifelong resident of Vegas, so I doubt she was in on it. Just in the wrong place at the wrong time. I have Warren running her through the system to see. Her name is Delinda Niles, lives in North Vegas."

"So was this place robbed the same as the last?" Earl asked.

"Yep, back door unlocked and the alarm shut down. Owner is blaming Delinda for leaving the door unlocked, but I told him it was a stretch to think that someone just happened to come by at that time to rob the place. Besides, one woman in the building alone at night, I'd be sure she would have had the doors locked."

~~*~~

"Damn it Ned, did you have to bring her back here?" Dark was scowling.

"I just thought she could be sold to the Arabs, she's not bad looking. Besides she saw us after Benny opened the back door."

"Our sales to the foreign buyers is over for now, we can't take her on the road with us. Just dispose of her, and do it quickly, we don't need any more prisoners."

"Okay boss, it'll be done. The desert here is so nice and big, they won't find her for a long while."

He left the trailer, Dark looked to Skeeter, "Is the auction going to go on as planned?"

"Yep, it's all arranged and everyone knows where to meet."

*

Chapter 18

The CSI supervisor, Larry Wayne, came over to Lynn and said, "Same as the other store, we got nothing, and the store's security tapes are all missing. We did find one camera that I think they missed outside, from across the street at a party store. I have my men over getting the tapes from them; maybe we'll have something to show."

"Thanks Larry, keep me informed if any of Dark's men show up on it." Larry agreed and went back into the jewelry store.

"Are you taking lead on this?" asked Ted Dresher, a detective from robbery, who was standing by listening.

"I'm sorry Ted, no, I'm just hoping to gather as much evidence on this crew to put them away for way too many crimes, but you have the scene, it's yours, but keep it under wraps until tomorrow." He agreed and went back to his men.

"If this Delinda turns up murdered, then it goes to homicide, so you may have an official stance on it," I offered.

"Not that I'm hoping for murder, but I'm in a gray area here. Weber is letting me take the case because he wants to see the boys returned and just about all the other department caseloads are heavy. Luckily there have been no murders in the city for a few days, freeing me up," she said with a grim smile.

"I guess my murder curse is taking a vacation," I laughed.

Lynn's cell phone rang and she answered, listened for a long pause and thanked the person on the other end. "That was Warren, he was running the check on Niles back in the squad room and a report came in, he took it since he was the only one in homicide, it seems they already found Niles, dead in the desert."

"How did they find her out there, it's a big desert?" Earl asked.

"It seems that two hikers were exploring for rocks out off the highway towards Boulder City when they saw a truck pull into the desert. Two men got out and pulled what looked like a woman from the back of the truck and put a bullet in her head. They drove off and the hikers went to the woman, she was dead of course. They called police and it came back to Warren in the precinct. It's now homicide, Dark is digging in deeper."

"When we get the boys back, you're going to have a ball nabbing Dark aren't you?"

"Bet your sweet bippy, his ass is going to be mine. Him and that whole damn carnival. I'll have all of our SWAT and backup to arrest the entire bunch of them. They don't come into Las Vegas and do this crap on my watch."

~~*~~

Dark Carnival Murders

Buck and Mac were back at the round-up and sweating in the heat, worse now today, it had climbed to over 110 degrees. Skeeter came up and said, "Good work last night, the women were prime beef for our investors, Dark was happy."

"Glad to oblige, we do our best," Buck replied.

"You still wanting to go with us tonight for the auction?"

"Sure, if we aren't going to get in the way."

"Oh no, you won't. We need extra men to help control the buyers; they get a little surly at times. They are a mean bunch. The two of you big men can keep them in their place."

"I love a good fight if it comes down to it."

"Hopefully not, just watch the men and if one of them gets a little heated, cool him down. When it comes to young boys, these perverts can get snarly."

"I'm sure Mac and I can handle it. Where's this all taking place?"

"I can't say right now, but we'll lead you there when it's time. The auction is taking place before we close down so you'll need someone to fill in for you. I'll arrange it, later." He turned and went off.

Buck was disappointed that Skeeter didn't tell him the location. He had the GPS tracker that Dave hid on him this morning after the jet plane incident, so he was prepared.

~~*~~

We took the half hour drive down to the area where the woman's body was found. The two hikers were sitting on the tailgate of their old army jeep that they brought over to the crime scene after they called the police.

"Did you get a look at the men?" Lynn asked them.

"Sorry, we were too far away to get a good look, they weren't very big though, kind of skinny and small looking. The woman was bigger than both of them but she was tied up."

"How about the truck?"

"It was a late model Ford pickup, it had a high cap covering the bed, like they used it to haul big things. It was blue and not very clean looking, well used I'd say. There was some kind of lettering on the front door, couldn't make it out. It was colorful though, with fancy lettering."

"Could it have said, Jacob Dark's Traveling Carnival and Wonder Show?" I asked.

"That's a mouthful, but it could have been. There was about the same number of words that you just said. It was kind of like carnival lettering, you know, fancy."

"Thanks, sorry to disturb your rock hunting, especially with a murder. Detective Warren will take your statements and you can go. We may need you again to identify the truck if we find it." Lynn turned to me and said, "I'll just bet I know where that truck is."

~~*~~

Angelo was enjoying the sightseeing that he and his mother were doing. They had gone up and down the strip to all the casinos and played a good number of games. Francis knew the odds were against her betting, but she enjoyed the action.

They had stopped at the McDonald's on the strip and were sitting with their food when Angelo's cell phone rang. The caller ID came up private but he answered.

"Yeah, Angelo DeMario here."

"Angelo, it's Benny Lesloe from Joisy City, can ya talk?" came the voice on his phone causing him to stiffen up.

"Yeah Benny whatcha need?" Francis gave Angelo a look, he just motioned not to worry.

"I understand that ya was lookin' for a creep named Lucius Cole? Whatcha need him for?""

"I don't need him, I was trying to get some info on him. Why you boys need to know?"

"We got a beef with him, his crew hit one of our fencing fronts for a ton of jewelry and we wants it back. You know where the mug is at."

"At this moment, no." Which was true, at that moment Angelo didn't know where Cole, AKA Dark, was at specifically. He didn't want to lie to the one friendly Mafia family that the Travianos dealt with. "Tell ya what Benny, I'll nose around out here and see what I can find, hows that with ya?"

"Good wit me Angelo, hows life with ya?"

"I'm sitting her with my mother having burgers and fries on the Vegas Strip. Isn't that nifty?"

"Sounds real nice, say hi to Francis for me, talk later." He hung up and Angelo put his cell away.

"What did that lowlife want?" Francis asked.

"It's the case my friends are on, the carnival man, they have a beef with him. I'm going to have to talk to Jim before I let Benny know where the creep is."

"Well if it's the man who kidnapped the children, let Benny know, that should take care of the creep."

Angelo laughed, "Mom, you always know how to deal with a situation don'tcha?"

"Mafia mothers always know what's best," she laughed then took a bite of her burger.

~~*~~

I was lounging in the precinct squad room with Earl waiting for our plan to start when my cell phone buzzed, it was Buck.

"What's the word?" I asked.

"I'm back in my phone booth so this will be quick. They aren't telling me where we go, just that we follow them so make sure the GPS guy is watching. We go earlier than closing, I don't know what time, so if I suddenly show we are leaving the carnival, that's the time. I may not be able to call so be ready. That's all I know or can say for now, so talk later, hopefully with three boys in tow." He hung up and I called over to Lynn in her office.

She came over, "What's up?"

I explained what Buck had said, and she looked concerned. "They won't tell them where they are going, that's worrisome. I think I need to put eyes on the carnival, just to be sure." She yelled for Warren, who was in the coffee room, he came out and over.

"Yeah Lieutenant?" he said.

"Being formal, is it time for promotions?"

"No, just saying it out of respect."

"Thank you, here's what I want you to do, take Williams and one other man and go sit on the carnival watching Buck and Dark. His picture is on my desk, watch them and if it looks like they are leaving the carnival grounds, get to me ASAP and then carefully follow them."

"I thought Buck had a tracker on?"

"For some reason I'm not trusting it and we have one chance to do this, or the boys will be gone."

"You got it, I'll take care of it." He went off after calling Williams from his desk.

"Better to be safe than sorry, I guess," I said.

*

Chapter 19

Angelo called next and told me about his contact with a Jersey mob looking for Dark. "Can you stall them off until tomorrow?"

"I already did, let me know what you want me ta do," he said.

"I will my friend, now enjoy your time with your mother and don't worry. I'll let you know how our sting goes tonight." He agreed and hung up.

I figured it wasn't something I needed to burden Lynn with, she already had enough worries without telling her the mob wanted Dark also. I leaned over and told Earl and he laughed.

"Boy, Dark is so screwed. You telling Lynn?"

"Oh hell no, you know her feelings about the mob. She's got enough on her plate with tonight. I may mention it after we finish this, maybe she'll reconsider and let the mob take Dark," I said.

"It will save the people of Vegas a lot of money in court costs and lawyer fees."

"Yes, it will. Maybe I'll tell Angelo to inform his friends to take care of all this."

"Hell, you're too moral to sick the mob on Dark, you prefer justice."

"We'll see," I said with a smirk.

"What are you two plotting over here?" Lynn asked as she came back to us.

"Just discussing politics. Nothing you'd be interested in," Earl said.

"Why is it I never trust what you say," she replied.

"Have you transferred your hostilities from Trapper to me now?"

"I'm still miffed about the stripper comment you made."

"Hey, I was just commenting on how you look good enough to get into the business."

Lynn opened her mouth but nothing came out, she took a breath and walked away.

"Hit a nerve, I'd say. Good move," I said.

"I'm so cool," he said with a smile.

~~*~~

Around six in the afternoon, Skeeter brought two men over to the round-up and told Buck they were his replacement.

"Time to go?" Buck asked.

"Almost, just one more thing to do. Follow me." He took Buck and Mac to one of the carnival semi-trucks in the area that they called the back yard, where the trucks were parked, and opened the back of the trailer. He turned and had a gun in his hand, "Okay boys, get in."

"What's this?" Buck demanded.

"It's about being cautious with your part in our scheme of things, Mr. Dark is being careful about the success of this mission tonight. Oh and hand over your cell phones."

Dark Carnival Murders

Buck stood defiantly and then Skeeter pointed his gun at Mac and fired into his leg. Mac screamed and went down. Buck went to him then looked to Skeeter.

"You son of a bitch, if you didn't have that gun I'd kick your fucking ass up through your mouth!" Buck yelled.

"Big talk for a big man, we suspect you aren't who you say you are, we also suspect you aren't cops so you must be into something we don't need to mess up our plans. Now the cell phones."

Buck pulled his phone out of his pocket and threw it a Skeeter. Skeeter ducked and it went past his head and into the field behind him. Skeeter looked back and said, "Okay, at least you don't have it. Now Mac's."

Buck pulled the cell phone from Mac and tossed it at Skeeter. He didn't want Skeeter to have them which is why he tossed them. Skeeter ducked again.

"Listen fucker, if Dark didn't want you alive, I'd love to shoot the both of you dead. Now get the fuck in the truck."

Buck was cursing in his mind, no sense in aggravating Skeeter any more than he already was.

He helped Mac up and they got into the truck. Skeeter closed the doors and put a padlock in the latch. Buck looked at Mac's wound, luckily it was only a graze. He didn't know if Skeeter was a lousy shot or planned the shot.

He stood and looked around the trailer, it was totally enclosed but there was a trap door in the ceiling towards the front that he couldn't reach, so he wasn't sure if it was secured. There was a skylight that provided enough light to see in the trailer. He couldn't reach the skylight either. This was not good, hopefully the GPS would show they were not moving and someone would come and let them out. He sat on the floor next to Mac and waited.

~~*~~

Warren called Lynn and said that Buck and Mac were replaced on their ride so something must be happening. Lynn thanked him and said to keep in touch. She called Dave in Electronics and he said that Buck had moved slightly from his ride, but then stopped in the lot away from the carnival. He was not moving, so something must be wrong. Lynn called Warren back and told him to carefully go see if he can find Buck in the parking area for the carnival trucks, Greg said he would, but she stopped him and asked if he had eyes on Dark.

"We can see his trailer, lots of men have gone in and out, but Dark hasn't left yet."

"Okay Greg, forget Buck for now, just watch Dark and his men and follow them if they move. I'll send a car to get Buck." She hung up and then called for someone to check on Buck's location.

Lynn called for her team to get ready to go out to the carnival and wait at Century 16 theatre for word as soon as she knew where they were going.

She turned to us and said, "Looks like something is going down. Shall we get out there?"

We stood and went to her unmarked car and she led the gaggle of patrol cars and SWAT out of the precinct parking lot. Everyone was tense, I could tell. Three boy's lives were at stake.

We drove down Vegas Boulevard to East Silverado Ranch Boulevard and she had everyone park in the Century 16 Theatre lot and wait for word.

Lynn called Warren and he said there still wasn't any movement, and he didn't see Buck or

Mac anywhere. Lynn said no problem, just keep watching.

~~*~~

Buck was pacing around the trailer and looking up at the two places that he could get out, if he could reach it. There was nothing in the trailer to climb up on.

"What are you thinking?" Mac asked.

"How I can get up there?" he said pointing to the closed openings.

Mac struggled to his feet and then clasped his hands and said, "Shall we do our circus act?"

Buck laughed aloud and came to the man putting his foot in Mac's hands as the big man boosted Buck up to the trap door. Buck was just able to reach it but it must have been locked from the outside, it wouldn't budge. He jumped down and they went to just below the skylight. Buck wasn't sure how to handle this but went up again. He pushed at the plastic cover it wouldn't budge. He kept pounding on the plastic but it wouldn't break. He came back down again.

"Damn, this is not good," he said then he heard a noise at the doors of the trailer; they went to the door and listened. It was someone at the back of the trailer; Buck figured it couldn't hurt so he started to yell.

He heard someone yelling back, "Who's in there?"

Buck wasn't sure who it may be, but he figured at this point it didn't matter. "Buck Carter and Mac Knight, we're being held prisoners. Who are you?"

"Stand away from the door," came the voice back. Buck and Mac went to the front of the trailer as they heard gun shots and then the door opened. It was Tim and another officer, they were grinning at them. "It was good we heard you banging on the trailer or we might have walked on by."

Buck said he was trying to get out and they jumped down from the trailer. Buck went over to where he threw his cell phone and the two cops helped to find the two phones.

They all went to the far edge of the lot where the patrol car was hiding, Buck helped Mac to manage walking to the cars and they got in. Ted radioed Lynn and said they had Buck.

~~*~~

"That is so good to hear, we're at Century 16, bring them down here." Lynn clicked off the radio and told us they had Buck and Mac. We all took a breath and then I asked if they had messed the deal.

"I have no idea, but we'll find out shortly."

We waited until the patrol car pulled up and Buck got out letting Mac rest in the car. "The fuckers locked us in a truck, they must know something is up. Do you have someone watching Dark?"

"We do, Warren and Williams are watching his trailer. Did they say why they suspected you?"

"Not really, they did say they didn't think we were cops so maybe they won't mess with the auction. It sounded pretty firm in its set-up. All you can do now is wait for Dark to make a move," Buck said.

"Dark will probably want to be at the auction, it's too important to him right now," I said.

"Okay everyone, we wait."

After about an hour of pacing, Lynn's cell phone rang, she answered, listened and then hung up. She smiled and yelled for her men to get ready.

Lynn turned to us and said, "Greg said Dark just got into his car and drove off, they're following him. It starts."

*

Chapter 20

Lynn was leading us by way of Warren's guidance on her cell. He reported that Dark was heading up Vegas Boulevard and just crossed over Desert Inn Road. A few seconds later, Warren confirmed that Dark had turned into the Riviera Hotel. Warren slowed his car to watch at a distance as Dark pulled into the valet parking and got out.

Lynn called her men and the captain of SWAT and told them where they were going. She then told Warren to get with hotel security and locate the room that Dark was using.

"Greg, it may be under Lucius Cole's name, check that also. Warn security we may be running a full blown attack on their hotel. Move fast."

We pulled into the long drive to the valet parking, blocking the way in. One car stopped at the road with flashers redirecting the traffic away from the hotel for now. Everyone piled out of the cars and into the lobby, startling the guests. Hotel security went full force to calm the people. The supervisor of the hotel cops came out to Lynn.

"Lieutenant, we have a quandary here, we can't legally give you personal info about the rooms unless you have a warrant."

Lynn got up to his face, "Listen chief, or whatever you are, there are three young boys about to be auctioned off to a group of perverts wanting to do unspeakable things to them once they take them out of your hotel. Do you have children?" Lynn demanded.

The man stood silently and then turned to the clerk at the counter and said to cooperate with the officers.

"Do you have a Jacob Dark or Lucius Cole registered?" Lynn demanded of the counter girl.

She punched keys on the computer and then said, "There is a Lucas Cole registered but no Lucius Cole."

Lynn reached over the counter and turned the computer screen towards her and studied the readout. She said, "It says he's from Gibsonton, Florida. The name is a typo, we got the room, 2060, second floor."

The team headed to the elevators, moving passengers out and cramming in the cars. Lynn hit the second floor button and waited. Earl and I were at the back of the elevator ready for anything, wanting to get the boys back to their families.

The elevators came to a stop and everyone flowed out to the door of the room. Lynn pushed her way through the men and up to the entrance. She put her ear to it and listened, she said she could hear nothing.

"Where's that hotel security chief?" She called back and he came forward. "Either open the door or we will bust it in."

He pulled his master door card and inserted it in the keycard lock, the door clicked and Lynn pulled him back. "Ready everyone," she said and pushed the door opened. Everyone burst into the room and stopped just short from the door. Lynn was startled to see Dark sitting on a couch all alone. She ran to him and pulled him off his seat and got in his face.

"Where are the boys, Dark?" She yelled at him.

He just stared at her, then said, "What boys? I'm waiting here for a female friend, who seems to be running late."

"Don't fuck with me Dark, or is it Cole. Talk now or I'll tear you apart!"

"I'm telling you officer, I don't know what you're talking about. I don't know anything about any boys."

Everyone was feeling helpless at this moment, I thought about something and stepped forward, moving up to Lynn still holding on to Dark.

I carefully pulled her away and said quietly in her ear, "Lynn you trust me don't you?"

She gave me a look and whispered back, "You have something?"

"I do but you aren't going to like it, do you trust me?"

"Jim, I know you want the boys back as much as I do, do you have something?"

"I do, but you don't need to know, can I have a moment with Dark, alone, no one in the room but him, Earl and I." I paused then said, "Please let me try something. Yes, I want the boys back and I would never gamble with their lives if I didn't think what I'm going to do wouldn't work. Trust me to try this."

She stood looking into my face then yelled for everyone to get out of the room. I signaled to Earl to come close, as everyone was going out to wait in the hallway.

Earl came up and asked me quietly, "What are you up to?"

"Get Angelo on your cell phone and then put him on speaker." Earl smiled and went off to dial Angelo.

I went to Dark and said, "Dark or Cole, whoever the hell you are, from the first day we met I didn't like you and I knew you had something to do with the kidnapping of the boys. You aren't fooling me or my police friends. We also know you are involved in jewel heists around the city and for the murder of a woman who was in the wrong place in one of the jewelry stores, we have witnesses. I don't care about all that, I care about three young boys whose lives you are ruining. I don't like that, and I don't like you. So you can tell me where the auction is going on or I have friends who would like to deal with you."

"You can threaten me with violence, I'll just have my lawyers put you away for brutality and I'll sue the cops for all this," he said quietly.

I looked to Earl and he nodded, coming up behind Dark. "Dark, this is my associate, a former CIA operative, now working with me to clean up scum like you. But he isn't the one you should be afraid of."

I went to Earl and he said Angelo was listening to the whole thing. I smiled and took his phone, "Angelo are you there?"

His voice came through loud and clear, "I sure is, Mr. R., what you want me to do?"

"Hang on for a moment," I went back to Dark. "The man on the other end of the phone is a friend of mine, Angelo, he is the son of the capo of the Traviano Mafia family out in New York. Ring any bells?"

Dark said nothing but I could see a light in his eyes.

"Okay, Angelo told me earlier that someone by the name of Benny Lesloe is interested in you. Does that ring a bell now?"

I definitely saw Dark's eyes go wide.

"There was a jewelry heist out in Jersey that you evidently had something to do with, and Lesloe is wanting you very badly for it. I asked Angelo to hold off telling Lesloe that you were here in Vegas, but I may reconsider that. Do you think your lawyers can protect you from the mob?"

I could almost see Dark's legs buckle a bit, he was definitely shaken by the news. "What do you want?" he said.

"Geez Dark, what have we been asking for? Where the hell are the boys? I'm giving you ten seconds to talk or I'll have Angelo call Benny."

Angelo helped by saying, "I got Benny on speed dial and I'll personally come out to hold Mr. Dark until Benny can send his men out to take him back to Joisey."

Good one Angelo. Dark turned pale.

"Nine seconds, eight, seven, six… times ticking Dark, what's it going to be? Tell me, or cement boots for you!"

"The cops won't let this happen!" Dark yelled.

"They want the boys back too. I'm sure they'll look aside as we take you out of here to a place where Angelo can hold you. They won't care about a pissant like you. Five, four, three…"

"Okay, okay, if you guarantee my safety, I'll tell!"

I looked to Earl and said, "Get Lynn."

He went to the door and called her back in. She came up and stood by.

"Mr. Dark, tell Lieutenant Carter where the boys are. Don't disappoint me. Angelo you still there?"

"Yes I am," came his voice from the cell phone. "I got my finger on the speed dial."

Lynn's eyes went wide and she said, "You brought the mob in on this?"

I looked to her and winked. Dark yelled, "Okay, I'll tell you where the boys are!"

Five minutes later Dark had given us the location of a warehouse where the auction was taking place. Lynn turned him over to her men and told them to escort him to the precinct and watch him carefully. I thanked Angelo and told him to relax for now, maybe we'd call Benny later. Lynn gave me the evil eye and then smiled.

"You did good, now don't tell me any more about it. We need to rescue the boys," she said.

We left the room as she was calling for full back up to go to the warehouse, and directed the SWAT team to the destination.

We drove up and over to Maryland Avenue and found the warehouse where the auction was going on. I was surprised that it was the same warehouse where Angelo and the porn actress were kidnapped back during the hypnotic murders. The parking lot had many expensive cars, telling us we had the right place. SWAT and Lynn's men covered the front door and the back.

Lynn went up to the entrance next to the big garage door and tried it. The door was locked. I was next to her and pounded on it. She gave me a look.

"What? They should answer," I said just as the door open and Lynn grabbed onto the man just inside and yanked him out. She signaled to her men and they all flowed into the room. I followed and saw what I hoped to see, the boys, alive and looking well.

*

Chapter 21

The warehouse was a tangle of cops in flak uniforms and assault rifles all aimed at a group of about a dozen men seated in folding chairs in front of a makeshift stage. The boys and three carnies were on the stage, one of the carnies grabbed one of the boys and held a gun to his head. I was working my way around the back of the platform in all the confusion. The men in the seats didn't move with all the fire power aimed at them.

"Yo shitface, let the boy go," Lynn yelled with her gun aimed at the man.

He sneered and said to make him. I came up behind him and hit him hard with the butt of my Glock. He went down as I turned the gun around and pointed it at the other two men as I grabbed the boys, pulling them back. Lynn came up on the platform along with Warren and seized the men, handcuffing them.

Lynn came over to where I had the boys and she knelt down to the youngest one. "We're the police and we're getting you out of here and back to your parents, how's that sound?"

The young boy looked worn and beat, but he smiled and nodded. Lynn yelled for Warren and Williams to take the boys to her car and watch them. They went out as Lynn went to the stage and yelled for silence.

"Okay all you perverts, you are all under arrest for pandering, child endangerment and pedophilia, the line forms to the left. Get moving now!"

They all grumbled but lined up. I was watching the procession just as Buck came flying in the door. He had taken Mac to LV Medical by way of Tim in his patrol car. Buck saw me and came over.

"Damn, you couldn't wait for me to start the attack?" he said.

"We got itchy. How's Mac?"

"He's going to be alright. He knew I wanted to be here so he chased me out of the hospital. Tim hotfooted it over here." Buck looked over to the three handcuffed men who were running the auction and I saw his eyebrows go up. He walked to the men and stopped in front of one of them.

"Well Skeeter, we meet again and you don't have a gun this time. That sort of evens us up." Buck brought his fist up and smashed Skeeter right in the face. "You're lucky I don't shoot you in the leg like you did Mac," he shouted down to the man now on the floor. He gave his famous grin and came back to me. "Damn that felt good. I've hated that man since I started working at the carnival. Hey, I can quit my job now," he laughed.

"Yep, you're back to work at our business. Did you call Lacey about Mac?"

"Hell no, she'll blame me for Mac getting shot. I don't want to incur her wrath when I go back to work."

"I'm sure Mac has already called her. We're lucky he didn't get killed," I said.

185

Dark Carnival Murders

Lynn came over and asked, "Jim, can you call the parents and have them come to the precinct to get their boys?"

"I'd be delighted, it is the highlight of this whole case." I went off to the side of the warehouse and called the Walkers first, then the Forents. It was a tremendous feeling to hear them expressing happiness that their boys were safe. They said they'd be down as soon as they could. I told them the boys were still with us and it would be about a half hour or more, so take care driving.

The perverts were all being led out to a couple vans that arrived, then Earl and I got in the car with the boys, Lynn was driving. The Forent boy sat in the front and we had the Walker boys between Earl and I. It was good that we had them, it would soon be over.

We arrived at the precinct and Earl and I led the boys to the squad room of homicide. Weber came in even though he was signed out, he wanted to greet the boys. The Walkers had already arrived and grabbed on to the boys as soon as they came through the door. The Forents came through the front entrance guided by an officer. They latched on to their son as soon as they saw him.

Mr. Walker came over and thanked me. "I can't take all the credit, Lieutenant Carter and her men did a great job on this also. Plus my men on the inside made it possible to track them down. It was a team effort. Now don't be too harsh on the boys for running off to the carnival, I'm sure they won't do that again."

He laughed and then Lynn said, "I have the names of a couple good counselors for the boys. I'm sure they'll need to talk to someone who can help them get over the ordeal."

"If the cost of the counselors is going to be a problem, let me know, I'll take care of it," I offered. "Now take your boys home, they look like they could use a nice hot bath."

The Walkers thanked us again and left. The Forents thanked everyone and left also. Weber congratulated everyone and he skittered out. It was now quiet in the squad room, it sounded nice.

All was right in the world now.

It was just after eleven in the evening. Lynn still had to take her men out to the carnival and close it down. She told me they'd have a bit of work ahead to sort out the good from the bad carnies. I had told her the carnival didn't own all the rides as they lease out space for private operators to set up their equipment. So not all the people were in on the criminal activities. Buck had told Lynn that they saw Dark with the jewelry in his trailer, she said they'd tear it apart.

I was really wearing down, so Earl and I left followed by Buck. I drove Earl back to his car and headed home. I drove in the drive and could hear the alarm going off. I guess Penny wanted to know when I got in. I parked the van and went into the kitchen nearly tripping over Willy who came bouncing into the room. I reset the alarm just as Penny came bouncing in also and latched on to me with a big wet one on the lips.

"That was nice, do you have an ulterior motive for such a greeting?"

"Lynn called and told me about finding the boys. She asked if I would remind you to come in tomorrow to file a statement about tonight and to bring Earl."

"It was nice of Lynn to spoil my surprise. So am I a hero now?"

"You're always a hero to me, Sweetie." She gave me a big grin then went off to the other room. I heard her yelling, "I'm heading to the bedroom, care to join me?"

I didn't think twice.

The next morning, Angelo was back in the kitchen cooking up a storm, I had dressed before going out because Penny warned me that Francis was here. I went to the kitchen and over to Angelo.

"Thanks Angelo, for what you did last night, it was really helpful in forcing Dark to give out the location of the boys."

He smiled and said, "All in a day's work."

I turned to Francis sitting at the snack bar with Penny, "Francis, you should be proud of your son, he helped save the boys."

"I always said my son was a good person. I'm very glad the boys are safe at home now."

"Yes, they are. What are you all plotting for today?"

Penny spoke, "We're going to my studio, I have a big name movie star on and Francis has agreed to be interviewed about her life. I'm trying to convince her to write a biography."

"Why not, everyone else is writing a book," I said just as my cell phone buzzed. It was Earl, I excused myself and went into the living room.

"What's up?" I asked.

"I came in to see Lynn to make my statement about our part in this mess and there was a bit of a commotion. Seems Dark was stabbed in his cell last night. Did Angelo call Benny?"

"I don't think so, but I'll ask. Is Dark dead?"

"Unfortunately no, he's in critical condition or so they are saying. Are you coming in soon?"

"Yeah, I'll be in shortly. Talk later," I said and hung up. I called to Angelo and he came in the living room.

"Yeah Mr. R.?"

"Angelo, you didn't let anyone know that we had Dark in custody did you?"

"No, never. You said to sit on it so I sat on it. Why?"

"Dark was shived in his cell this morning, he's critical but alive."

"Wasn't me who ratted him out, although I would have liked to."

"Same here, okay I have to go in and see Lynn. Take care of the women." I stuck my head in the kitchen and said I had to go save the world and would see them later. I went to my van and drove out.

Lynn and Earl were in her office when I got there. "Did your mob buddies have something to do with this?" she yelled at me when I got to the door.

"Not guilty, Angelo says he was mum about it. Could be someone in there who didn't like child abductors?"

"We're figuring that. They put him in general population instead of in solitary. I didn't know, too late now."

"Whatever, they didn't finish the job, he survived," Earl said.

*

Chapter 22

We finished making out our statements and then Lynn treated us to something out of the lunchroom machines. Big spender.

"We went through all of Dark's office and found most of the jewelry. He really wasn't all that smart, but he had a track record of jewelry heists. From what I hear from Bill Kestor, this is the only time he's been caught. Also seems they did slip in the little person and he hid in the store until closing, then he would disable the alarm and open the back door."

"See, I was right," Earl beamed.

"Yes Earl, you were. It's good you're on our side," Lynn mugged. "We got the two hikers in this morning and they identified the truck from the carnival lot, so we got Dark for the murder also. All nice and tidy."

"So what's going to happen to the carnival?" Earl asked.

"We let all the people go who could prove they were just leasing space from Dark to set up their rides and the rest of the equipment will stay until we can figure out what to do with it. They pretty much pulled up stakes this morning and are mostly gone, leaving only a few rides that were owned by the business."

"Are the sideshow freaks and geeks gone too?" I asked.

"All but Ben, the little person, and a couple other carnies that Ben ratted out for a deal. He'll still go away for robbery but in a friendlier prison than here, he wouldn't survive in our jails."

Lynn's phone rang and she answered, listened and then hung up. "News flash, Clark County won't be footing the bill for Dark's trial and his stay in jail, he just bit the big ride in the sky. They said his internal bleeding was worse than they thought and couldn't save him."

"I'm not sad, he deserved what he got," I said. "If we're finished here, I need to go to the office to see if Lacey is having fits because Mac got shot. I hope she doesn't tear the place apart too badly." I stood and Earl said he was going also.

"Hey guys, thanks again. It's always a pleasure working with you," Lynn said.

We were back at the office building and parked. Earl exited his car and followed me in the back door. We carefully entered as the cow bell on the door clanged and then I waved to the camera, but Lacey popped out of the storeroom next to the back door with a scream and scared the hell out of me.

"Gotcha!" she said with a laugh.

"You're in a good mood for almost losing a husband," I said when my heart slowed.

"Yes, but I didn't and that makes it all the better. He came home last night and we celebrated his victory over the bad guys. He's resting today, I wore him out," she said with a smirk.

"I'll just bet he's worn out, three days without him must have been tough."

"I managed. Now you have some people in the front who want to see you." She walked away and Earl and I went up front. We came into the inner lobby and found the Walkers sitting on the couches.

"What do we owe this visit?" I said.

"Just stopped by to say thank you again, and apologize for being pains in the neck," Mr. Walker said as they all stood.

"Pains, never. Just concerned parents." I looked to the boys who were a lot cleaner than I last saw them. I turned to Lacey and asked, "Lacey, where's Willy?"

"He's in your office sleeping on your chair," she replied.

I turned to the boys and said, "Go down that hallway to the second door on the left and wake up my dog. Be careful he's small and fragile." They both smiled and went off.

"You may lose your dog, but I'll make sure they leave him here," Mr. Walker said. "We also stopped to say we talked to a social worker who deals with abused and troubled children, it won't cost us anything since it's government funded and I qualify for aid. Thank Detective Carter for recommending them. The social worker talked to the boys and they seem to have taken it in stride, but we will be watching them."

"Good, I hope it all works out." I could hear laughter and little yips from my office and then Willy came running out and over to me. I picked him up as the boys followed him out.

Mrs. Walker reached over and petted Willy and asked the boys if they'd like a dog also? They bounced around and replied that they did.

"Well, you can't have mine. My wife would kill me if I gave him away."

Mrs. Walker looked to her husband and said "We'll go look in the pound and have everyone pick out a dog."

We all said our good-byes and they left. I watched them go to their car and the boys hardly looked like they went through a harrowing experience. I put Willy down and went to my office followed by Earl.

"I could use a nice cheating husband case right now, the kind where I sit in a parking lot spying on him," Earl said as he sat in my client chair.

"You'd just fall asleep."

"Me? Never, I do my job and do it well. Do you think you'd be interested in purchasing one used carnival?"

I gave him the finger and he laughed, "You have no sense of adventure."

"You buy the carnival, then you can be the whole freak show."

Buck popped his head in the door, "Hey guys, what's up?"

"Just unwinding, are you getting out of your carnie mode and back into security?"

"I have to retrain my men, they were all goofing off while I was gone, it's good to be back," he said and went to his office.

"Yes, it's very good for everyone to be back," I said and sat back in my chair.

THE END

For every ending there's a new beginning.

Enjoy a preview of the next book, "Lipstick Murders"

Chapter 1

The woman was reclined as her make-up was being applied. The foundation had been smoothed out on her silky skin and then rouge was added for color. Mascara was spread across her eyelashes, and then liner to bring out her eyelids. The person doing the make-up was looking through the various lipsticks in the make-up kit, to decide which color would make her look pouty and sexy. A deep shade of red was selected and applied to her lips. It was then smeared over her cheeks and finally the red was streaked over each eye. She now had a face that looked like the Joker from the Batman movie. She didn't care, she was dead.

~~*~~

I was relaxing in my office waiting for Lacey to come bombing in, telling me there was an emergency that needed my attention. She loved to startle me whenever a person came in looking for a private investigator. I had a good staff and associates, Trapper and Earl, both very competent investigators, but a bit goofy at times. It was something that broke up the tension of dealing with missing children or murder.

My good friend and business partner, Buck, took care of the security guard part of our business. He now had about a hundred and sixty men on his roster, all guarding various businesses in and around Las Vegas. I had moved my lovely wife, and now Vegas' favorite talk show host, Penny, out to Vegas to live. She fell in love with the town on our earlier visits. After we came out, Buck, Trapper and then Earl all joined us in Sin City. We left Michigan with all the snow and cold, for the hot, sunny life in Vegas. I never regretted the move. Neither did Penny.

I was suddenly startled by a tug on my pant leg. I looked down to see Willy, our toy Yorkie, pulling on my pant cuff. I smiled and reached down to pet him and pull him off my cuff. I hadn't seen him come into the room; he was so small and easy to miss. Now Penny wasn't so easy to miss, as she came in the office. She was a beautiful woman for her age. Not that I complain about age, I was now sixty-three and still feeling like thirty. Age doesn't mean a damn thing when you're trapped in an older body. Penny was a couple years younger, but looked like she was in her forties, and still sexy as ever.

"What were you daydreaming about?" she asked me, as she sat in the client chair at my desk.

"You in a bikini," I joked, as I looked to the poster of her in a bikini, on my wall. I had it made from a picture I took while we were on a ship cruise that resulted in murders.

"I'm glad you have that poster, so you don't daydream about any other woman. Are you working on a case?" she asked.

"No, I'm bored here, thinking about going out for lunch. Want to join me?"

"I think you should wait for Lacey to tell you that there is a client in the lobby."

I was surprised about that, and wondered why Lacey hadn't called me yet. Lacey suddenly came flying in my door.

"Jim, you have a person out here and he needs help. I should tell you that he is hunky and handsome. He's a model!" she beamed and went back out.

Penny smiled and said, "I almost stayed in the lobby to watch his cute butt, but I saw Willy coming in here, so I followed."

"Cute butt? What's wrong with my cute butt?"

"Yours is cute too, but there's so much more of it." She smiled, as I stood.

"Are you insinuating I have a large butt?" I protested, as I headed towards the door.

"I'm not insinuating, I'm stating, you have a large butt."

I kissed her on the head and left the room. She followed on my heels.

I went through the glass doors to the lobby and saw him, he was hunky and handsome. I hated him right off. "May I help you?" I asked Mr. Wonderful.

Penny went behind him in the lobby and I could see she was checking out his body. He was wearing a red t-shirt and tight white jeans. I gave her a look and she smiled back to me.

"Mr. Richards, you were referred to me by a former client of yours, Stacey Trent," the Adonis said.

Dark Carnival Murders

I cringed hearing the name, remembering her from the Black Widow murders. Her husband was killed by the spiders, and then we suspected her of the crime. She later proved to be innocent, but she was still a wacko.

"I remember her well. Shall we go to my office to talk?"

He followed me and then I pointed out my door, stopping to block Penny from following.

"You don't need to be in there. Go bother Lacey or something," I said as I went to the office, watching her in the hallway giving me dirty looks. I smiled to her, waved and closed the door. I knew that was going to bite me in the large butt later.

"Now, you are?"

"Barry Polander, I'm a model for the Lansome Modeling Agency. I do photo shoots for men's clothing and runway work when needed."

"So, why do you need a private investigator?"

"Actually, I don't. I need a bodyguard. I understand that you have people who protect celebrities."

I wondered how he figured he rated as a celebrity, but he must have money, so I wouldn't feel bad taking some of it. "Yes, we do have bodyguards to watch over celebrities. Why do you feel you need one?"

"Have you seen the news this morning?"

"Sorry, I haven't seen the newspaper yet, or watched TV. What was there that I should know?"

"Tiffy Blumquest, the runway model, was murdered sometime last night. And threats were made to other models. I'm not taking chances, so I came to you."

"I see. I'll have to talk to a couple friends of mine on the LVMPD about the murder. How soon do you want to start?"

"As soon as possible, I have a career to think about, and I make good money at it."

I liked hearing that. "Okay, I have a person who would do well for you," I said thinking about Angelo, my former mob enforcer friend, who moved here from New York and started working for us. "He's someone who will not let anyone near you that you don't want."

"Is he tough?"

"Let me just say he used to be a leg breaker for a mob family out in New York. Is that tough enough?"

He got a big smile and said, "I like that. I'm from New York, would I know of the family?"

"Traviano, does that ring a bell?"

His eyes went wide, "Wow, yes. When do I get to meet him?"

"Hold on," I said as I went to the door and out. I went down to Buck's office and found Angelo relaxing in a chair on the side of the room. Buck was behind his desk doing paperwork, which he hated, but it had to be done. Angelo saw me and stood.

"Mr. R, good ta see ya dis morning." He was breaking back into his pattern of mob talk. Then he smiled and said, "I'll rephrase that, how are you this morning?" he grinned. "I'm trying to refine myself, I am rubbing elbows with famous people now."

I knew his job had put him guarding a number of really big celebrities who came to visit Vegas, so he had to project a better image.

"Angelo, you sound very refined. I have a case for you, if Buck has nothing else for you?"

Buck spoke, "You can have him, I've got nothing."

"Thanks. Follow me then." He came out after me and to my office. We went in and I introduced him to Barry. They shook hands, as Barry was looking surprised at the size of Angelo.

"Good to meet you, Barry," Angelo said. "You need protection, from whom?" he said with perfect diction.

They sat as Barry explained the murder and his concern. Angelo sat listening and then smiled.

"No, problem. I won't let you get hurt in any way. But you have to listen to me when I give an order to do something, like get behind me."

"I can do that, I don't need to be murdered. Are we good to go?" Barry asked.

"Sure, just stop on the way out to give the retainer to my receptionist and you can leave. You can be sure that Angelo is the man for your needs." I was sounding like a commercial.

They went out and I sat back in my chair as Penny came storming in. She closed the door and came over to sit on my lap. "Feel like fooling around?" she asked.

"In the office? How tempting. Or are you horny from seeing the Greek God?"

"Well, he may have given me the idea, but you know he could never replace you."

"I think you'd try. But there is no replacing me."

My door flew open and in walked Trapper. "Oops, am I interrupting something?"

"I think a closed door means that you are interrupting something," I said.

"Sorry, but I got a call from my gal Sam, she's invited me to go out of town with her, and I wanted to let you know."

"Okay, you've told me, now go and let us go back to what we were doing."

He went out and I reached over to my desk intercom and called Lacey. "Hold my calls and I'm now unavailable. Watch Willy and don't let me be disturbed."

"Okay, but you and Penny need to keep the noise down," she laughed and hung up.

*

Continued in the book…

~~*~~

Jim Richards Family of Readers

Thanks to the following people who are now part of the Jim Richards Family of Readers. They have read a book or more and enjoyed them. They all volunteered to be included in the list. If you are a fan of the books, send me your full name and you will be included in future books. Send your name to murdernovels@bobmoats.com to be added here and on the website.

* Achim Feifel * Al Norris * Alex Wheatley * Alexandra Delporte-Wilkinson * Amy Tapia * Andrea Bryan * Anne Shepherd * Arianda Sugar * Arlene Markowski * Ashley Augustus * Audra Hall * Barbara Hughes * Barbara Sammons * Barbara Schuler * Barbara Zirger * Beth Donohue Plenskofski * Betsy Childress * Beth Gibson * Bill Sandy * Bill Tornquist * Billie-jo Collie * Boni J Rychener * Carl Bishopric * Carla Lewis * Carole Henderson * Carolyn Conroy * Carolyn Riddle-Linington * Cassy Bailey * Cathie Turner * Chad Hudson *

Dark Carnival Murders

Charlotte L Duran * Cheryl L. Everett * Cindy Ackley Nunn * Cindy Valstad * Connie Bancroft * Corinne Kay O'Daniel * Dana Robbins Chuchran * Dana Wichita * Danielle Monique * Darren Heald * Dave Travers * David Wilkinson * DeAnn Jannereth * Deanna Miller * Deb Breuker Balbo * Debbie Carter * Debbie White * Deborah Fartuch * Deborah Gauze * Deborah Sullivan * Dee King * Denise Freeman * Diana Carver * Dixie Beck * Donna Gould * Donna Thompson * Donny Minter * Doris Kight * Eddie Moore * Eric Walters * Felicia Annette Bradfield * Francine Menor * Gail Chesney * Georgiann Minster * George Conner * Greg Colucci * Hayley Rankin * Harold Garcia * Heidi Arnold * Irma Ranee Coy * Jacqueline Moss * Jan Kimball * Janice Schneider * Janice Spoor * Jennifer Redmond * Jessica Keown-Belous * Jim Beck * Jo Boguslaw * Jo Turner * Joanne Marie Turner * John Peiffer * John Wisbiski * Joseph Wauro * Joyce Stacy * Joyce Trifiletti * Judy Franklin * Judy Travers * Judy Padgett * Julie Heath * Junnahvee Benson * Karen Dahl * Karen Grams * Karen Higham * Karen Kaiser * Karen Meinburg Richwine * Karen Kirkman Parker * Karin Hawkins * Karin Vasvari * Kathleen Donohue Roesing * Kathleen Riddle-Wolfe * Kathy Hinds Moore * Kathy Jones * Kathy Mitchell * Katie Benzler * Kay Burns * Kelly Garcia * Ken Boggs * Keota Rodriguez * Kiera Mccarthy * Kim Estes * Kitty Stolle * Kristie Sciler * Kirsty Stanton * LaLonnie Scallen * Larry Morris * Leann Parr * Lenora Scales * Leslie Marie Jackson * Linda Forester * Linda Ingle Cox * Linda Kennerö * Linda Magill * Lisa Bower * Liz Gibson * Lorraine Wiman * Loretta Alexander * Lynda Bowles * Lynette Lawrance * LuAnn Louttit * Manny Rothman * Marcia Gibson DeWitt * Marie Calder * Marlene Bryan * MaryLouise Kramp * Mary Lynn Gross * Megan Atkins * Meghan Hyden * Melody Cannavan * Michael Carruthers

* Michael Dinkens * Michael Vannoy * Michelle Burns-Mitchell * Michelle Pilcher * Micki Potter * Mike Moats * Mimi Baur * Myrna Hecht * Nadine Sutton * Nancy Ellen Sayre * Natalie Quine * Neena Martin * O'Della Wilson * Pat Pollington * Pat Rohn * Patricia Jarmon * Patricia C Trezza * Patrick Barry * Paul Lawrance * Peggy Davis * Phyllis Bassett * Raylene Matheny * Rebecca Collins Besner * Renee Brumley * Reta Hanna * Reta Moats * Roberta Navarro-Harder * Sally Berneathy * Sally Hubler * Sarah Santos * Satka Nikc * Sharon E. Edwards * Sharon Mangini * Sharon McMillon * Sheena Rawl * Sherry Amstutz * Shirley Alvarez * Shirley Davies * Shirley Williams * Stacie Rowe * Stephanie Conner * Steve Cullen * Susan Haughton * Susan Hesse Adams * Susan Salomon * Suzan K Chase * Taisha Cullum * Tamara Moore * Tammy Castleberry * Tammy Lynn Wood * Ted Murphy * Terri Atkins * Terri Creech * Terry Raab * Tonia Rachael Riggs-Williams * Travis Fleury-Lopez * Twyla Gawlas * Val Brooks * Walt Munsel * Yvonne Isakson *

Thank you to all these wonderful people.

Thank you for purchasing this book. I hope you enjoy it as much as I enjoyed writing it for my faithful readers. Please feel free to email me to tell me what you thought about my stories. I love hearing from the readers. I can be reached at murdernovels@bobmoats.com thanks again!

www.ingramcontent.com/pod-product-compliance
Lightning Source LLC
Chambersburg PA
CBHW070835120626
46556CB00002B/761

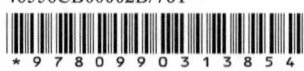